"Nick, don't be vulgar."

Even as Jenny chastised him, the admiration in his eyes gave her a heady feeling.

"It's not vulgar to look." He walked slowly toward her. "I'm not so sure that touching's vulgar, either. Shaking hands isn't vulgar, is it?"

Jenny peered up at him, barely hearing his words. Intoxicating desire engulfed her, tugged her toward him.

"And then there's the social kiss," Nick continued hypnotically. His lips brushed ever so lightly over her soft cheek. "Of course, really good friends might add a touch like this...." He reached out and slowly traced the curve of her breast.

Jenny sucked in her breath as waves of longing surged through her. She strained against his hand. "I can't stand much more of this, Nick."

"Sure you can," he said, suddenly swinging her up in his arms. "Don't underestimate yourself."

Judith McWilliams finds life as a full-time writer, wife and mother of four incredibly hectic but sometimes inspiring. In *Honorable Intentions*, her fifth Temptation, Judith drew on her own experience as the mother of a near genius for her portrayal of the lovable Jed. "The problem with kids like that," Judith says, "is that you end up embarrassed sometimes because you never know what they're going to say."

Currently Judith's life is more hectic than usual because her family is in the process of moving to Indiana from New York State.

Books by Judith McWilliams

HARLEQUIN TEMPTATION

78–POLISHED WITH LOVE
103–IN GOOD FAITH
119–SERENDIPITY
160–NO RESERVATIONS

Honorable Intentions

JUDITH McWILLIAMS

Harlequin Books

TORONTO • NEW YORK • LONDON
AMSTERDAM • PARIS • SYDNEY • HAMBURG
STOCKHOLM • ATHENS • TOKYO • MILAN

Published December 1987

ISBN 0-373-25284-6

Printed in Canada

"OH, GOD." Jenny Ryton carefully set the inventory sheet she was holding on the counter and ran her suddenly damp palms down her corduroy-covered thighs.

"What's the matter?" Marge mumbled around the pins in her mouth. "Did the company miscount the number of bolts they sent again?"

"She's here." Jenny nodded fatalistically toward the dark blue car pulling into the parking lot in front of her quilt shop.

"She?" Marge spat out the pins and peered myopically through the large multipaned window. "Which she?"

"Miss James, the caseworker from Social Services." Jenny's voice was tight with suppressed tension. "When I called her last Friday to ask why it was taking so long for them to come to a decision about Jed's custody, she said she hoped to have an answer for me this week."

"Don't you worry none." Marge patted Jenny's clenched fist comfortingly. "Of course they'll give you custody of Jed. Haven't you had him for the past four years? Didn't his own grandmother give him to you?"

"Unfortunately, as Social Services has already pointed out, his grandmother didn't have any legal right to give him to me." Jenny swallowed, trying to ignore her stomach's nervous churning. *Please let it be good news.* She sent up a hasty prayer. *Don't let them take Jed away.* She loved him so much. It was only at times like this that she even remembered he was the son of her heart instead of her body.

"No right!" Marge's middle-aged features set in outrage. "She's the boy's own flesh and blood, isn't she? His only living relation!"

"But she never went to court and got legal custody," Jenny repeated tautly. She glanced around the empty store. "Why don't you take your lunch break now, Marge? It's almost noon, anyway."

"If you're sure?" Marge peered uncertainly at the case-worker, who was opening the door.

"Yes, I'm sure. Go ahead. Miss James won't be here that long."

"How long does it take for her to tell you you can adopt Jed?" Marge gave Jenny an encouraging smile before slipping out through the back room.

"Good morning, Miss James." Jenny braced her body as if for a blow. She had a bad feeling about this visit. A feeling that had been growing over the past month as Social Services had dragged their feet about reaching a decision.

"Yes, it is. I just love these early-September days—so crisp and clear. They always make me think of bonfires and marshmallows," she gushed.

Jenny's heart began to pound at the woman's stilted manner. She could almost feel the regret and embarrassment emanating from Miss James.

"Such lovely material this is." Miss James fingered one of the bolts of cloth piled on the counter. "I really like paisley prints. Especially in brown."

"It's part of the Museum Collection from VIP," Jenny supplied automatically, willing the woman to quit dithering and get to the point.

As if responding to Jenny's silent demand, Miss James set her purse on the counter and cleared her throat. "I wish I had better news for you, Miss Ryton, but after a great deal of thought my superior and I have decided that Jed will be better off in the long run with the Devlins."

Jenny listened to the words echoing through the empty shop while a giant fist seemed to be squeezing all the blood from her heart. Her pale skin lightened alarmingly, causing the dusting of freckles across her small nose to stand out in stark relief. It had happened. She was going to lose Jed. But not without a fight! She wasn't going to smile bravely and simply hand him over. She was going to oppose Social Services all the way. Jenny expelled her breath in deference to the buzzing in her ears and made a valiant attempt to respond rationally.

"May I ask what you based your decision on? Certainly not on the wishes of his grandmother. And most assuredly not on Jed's."

"Mrs. Foster has no legal say in the matter," Miss James replied calmly. "And while we certainly take a child's feelings into account, they are by no means our sole criterion. Miss Ryton, please don't take this personally."

"Don't take it personally!" Jenny's unnatural calm exploded. "You come waltzing in here and tell me that you've decided I'm not fit to raise a child, and then you tell me not to take it personally! How the hell should I take it?"

"It's not that you aren't fit to raise a child. It's simply that you aren't the best parent for this particular child. Miss Ryton, Jed has an IQ of 187!" she said in an awed tone. "Do you have any idea what that means?"

"It means that he gets up to some very creative mischief," Jenny said dryly.

"It's no joking matter," Miss James reproved. "He's a genius. He needs constant mental stimulation if he's to reach his potential."

"Wrong!" Jenny snapped. "He's a nine-year-old boy who needs love if he's ever going to realize his God-given potential."

"The Devlins can give him that stimulation." Miss James ignored her outburst. "He's a college professor and she writes children's books."

"That attitude, Miss James, borders on intellectual elitism," Jenny bit out. "I certainly don't envy you trying to defend that stand in court."

"In court?" Miss James looked taken aback.

"Did you really think that I wouldn't contest your arbitrary decision? You're proposing to take Jed out of a home where he's been happy for the past four and a half years—not only been happy, but thrived physically and mentally—and hand him over to a pair of strangers."

"They aren't strangers, Miss Ryton," Miss James inserted. "Jed has met them."

"And been singularly unimpressed!" Jenny retorted. "As you would have found out if you'd bothered to ask him. According to Jed, Mrs. Devlin's main concern seemed to be whether or not he tracked mud on her prize oriental carpets."

"Just teething pains," Miss James insisted. "She isn't used to small boys. Once she is—"

"She could quite likely wind up hating them! For heaven's sake, why don't you either find the woman a nice neat little girl or, better yet, a baby that she can train from the beginning not to breathe too heavily around her precious antiques."

"Actually, they did apply for an infant, but when we had to tell them that they were facing at least a five-year wait and at the end of five years they'd be too old to qualify for a baby..." She sighed. "I know it's not the ideal home for Jed, but both my supervisor and I honestly believe that in the long run it will be best for him."

"Simply because Mr. Devlin has a Ph.D? And in medieval poetry of all things!" Jenny said scathingly.

"Miss Ryton, I know you're disappointed...." Miss James purposefully picked up her purse. "But everything else aside, the Devlins have one tremendous plus in their favor. They can offer Jed a male role model. Something that no single woman, no matter how well-intentioned, can do."

Jenny frowned. "Male role model?"

"Yes." Miss James nodded. "And that will become increasingly important as Jed reaches puberty. Everything else we could have overlooked, but not that."

"Well, I may not be married yet, but I'm planning to be in the near future." Jenny heard the words emerge with numbed detachment. Mrs. Devlin wasn't the only one who dabbled in fiction, Jenny thought, biting back a hysterical urge to laugh.

"You're going to be married!" Miss James gasped. "But why didn't you say so?"

"You didn't ask," Jenny replied in perfect honesty. "Besides, at the time neither had I been asked."

"But this changes everything," Miss James said in some confusion. "I'll have to check with my supervisor, but under the circumstances I don't see why—" She broke off as the door to the shop opened.

Jenny glanced up, her heart sinking as she recognized Nora Fleming. Oh, no! The town's most inveterate gossip. If Nora learned that Jenny was supposed to be engaged, all of Litton would know before nightfall.

"Um, Miss James." Jenny leaned closer and whispered, "I'd appreciate it if you didn't say anything about this for a few days. You see," she improvised, "he just asked me last night and I want to tell my parents first before we make a public announcement. They live in a retirement community in Florida. If this got around, one of my folks' friends might call to congratulate them and they'd be so hurt if they hadn't already heard the news from me."

"You can count on my discretion." Miss James beamed happily at her. "But I can tell my supervisor, can't I?"

"Certainly." Jenny cast a cautious eye at Nora, who had recognized the caseworker and was sidling closer in hopes of overhearing something worth repeating.

"Don't you worry about a thing, Miss Ryton. I'm just so happy that everything is going to work out without us having to resort to anything as unpleasant as a court battle." She shuddered. "Give me a call as soon as you contact your parents."

"I will." Jenny smiled weakly, walking the caseworker to the door.

My God, what have I done? Jenny watched the woman cross the parking lot with a feeling of impending doom. The only thing she *could* do, she assured herself. If a husband was what it took to keep Jed, then a husband she would have. But what husband and from where was he supposed to come?

Frantically she tried to conjure up the name of an eligible candidate, but her mind remained discouragingly blank. Litton was a small town. Little more than a village. It didn't contain all that many men, let alone marriageable ones. But she'd find a husband. She pressed her soft lips together in grim determination.

"Bad news?"

She jumped at the sound of Nora's shrill voice.

"What?" Jenny turned to the avidly watching woman.

"Wasn't that the caseworker from the county who's looking into Gemma's grandson's case?"

"Yes, that was her. What may I do for you this morning, Nora?" Jenny deliberately changed the subject, and Nora, with a final frustrated glance through the window at the caseworker's disappearing car, accepted it.

"It's about that quilt I finished piecing last week. I decided I want to use a russet print for the backing. What do you have?" She glanced around the well-stocked shelves.

"This just came in this morning." Jenny reached down behind the counter and pulled up a bolt of cloth still wrapped in cellophane.

"New?"

"Brand-new. It's part of Gutcheon's American Classics Collection." Jenny ripped off the protective covering. "You're the first person in town to even see it," she encouraged, knowing Nora's penchant for being first.

"Hmm." Nora put on her bifocals. Digging some material swatches out of her purse, she began to compare them with Jenny's fabric. "It matches," she decided. "I guess it'll do. Give me seven yards."

"You've made a good choice." Jenny began to clear off the cutting table.

"That's quite a shipment you got in today." Nora fingered a dark green broadcloth. "Speaking of things getting in, you wouldn't have heard anything from Angie, would you?"

"Angie?" Jenny muttered distractedly, trying to find a clear space to drop the bolts.

"Amy and John Carlton's youngest. You were always as thick as thieves with her when you were both in school. She married that Stephanos boy and moved to South Carolina."

"North Carolina. Her husband teaches at Duke, although at the moment they're on sabbatical in New Zealand. I haven't had a letter from her since last month. Why?"

"I was just wondering if she might have said anything about her brother."

"Nick?" Jenny began to measure the material Nora had chosen. "Last time she mentioned him was when he turned thirty-nine in June. She said he was in the Middle East somewhere."

"Well, he ain't no more," Nora related with satisfaction. "He's right here in Upstate New York. I saw him not half an hour ago as I came by the old Carlton farm. Lordy." Nora sighed. "I never thought to see a Carlton in that place again. Not after Nick ran away to join the navy and his father was killed by that drunk driver."

"He didn't run away," Jenny said dryly. "His cousin Sam drove him to the bus station."

"You always did know exactly what was going on in that family, didn't you? Nice girl, Angie. Not at all like her brother. Wild he was. Wild as the devil."

"On occasion." Jenny reached for the scissors and began to cut the cloth. "But he could be kind, too. I remember once when I was in high school and he was home on leave. David and I were in Franco's Restaurant to celebrate winning some football game or other. When the bill came, poor David realized he didn't have enough money to pay it." A reminiscent smile curved her lips. "We were sitting there counting and recounting our money in the hope that it had somehow multiplied, when suddenly Nick came up and greeted David like a long-lost brother. He shoved a bill at David and said that he'd been looking for him to return the twenty dollars he'd borrowed."

"Borrowed?" Nora frowned.

"He hadn't really borrowed it. It was simply a way for Nick to give David the money without embarrassing him in front of the other diners. David was so grateful. To say nothing of me." She chuckled. "I had visions of us spending the rest of the night washing dishes."

"It's a shame poor David had to go die in Vietnam."

"A damn shame." For a brief second bitterness filled Jenny, but she resolutely shook it off. "That'll be $21.72."

Nora handed her the money. "Did he ever make good?"

"Who?" Jenny asked absently as she opened the cash register.

"Nick Carlton!" Nora said impatiently.

"I don't know. Angie never mentioned it. There you are." She handed Nora her package and change. "Be sure to bring in the quilt when you get it finished. I'm anxious to see how it turned out."

"Be glad to." Nora bustled out.

Jenny carefully refolded the material on the bolt. Poor Nora. She smiled ruefully. The woman hadn't gotten much information out of her. Not that she had any to give. Jenny hadn't seen Nick in ages. Not since his father's funeral nearly twelve years before, and that had been only a fleeting glimpse as she hadn't wanted to intrude on the family's grief. After that Angie had married and left town and Mrs. Carlton had moved to Arizona, so there had been nothing to bring him back to Litton. Certainly not the farm his family had worked for six generations. Although as far as she knew, he still owned it. Had Nick come home to work the property the way his father had always wanted him to do? Somehow she couldn't see him as a farmer. He'd always been such an unsettled person. Always restlessly searching for what lay over the next hill. But her memories were from many years ago. Who knew what he might . . .

Jenny suddenly dropped the bolt of cloth she was holding. Of course! That was it! Nick Carlton could be the answer to all her problems. It seemed almost providential. She needed a husband and suddenly Nick appeared. But had he appeared alone? He could have brought a wife with him.

But if he hadn't . . . If he had remained unmarried, then there was a possibility she could convince him to help her. And as long as there was that possibility, no matter how slim, she had to explore it.

How could she go about discovering if he was free? Her brown eyes focused blankly on a rack of purple-hued fabric. Subtlety was what was called for, she decided. She'd get a pie out of the freezer and take it over to the Carlton farm as a housewarming gift. Then if Nick did have a wife, she could give her the pie and escape. But if he didn't . . . If he was there by himself . . . A rising sense of excitement spiraled through her. She'd go just as soon as Marge returned. Time was of the essence. She wouldn't be able to stall Miss James for long. Within a few days she was going to have to come up with a husband. And she would, she vowed recklessly. No matter what it took, she would. Jed was worth any sacrifice.

Jenny spent the short car ride out to the Carlton farm mentally trying out and rejecting various approaches. She couldn't seem to come up with one that didn't make her sound like some kind of a nut.

"Welcome back, Nick." Her words echoed brightly in the car's interior. "I'm so glad you've come home because it just so happens that I need a husband on short notice." Jenny winced. She could never carry off bluntness of that magnitude. No, she decided. She'd have to sneak into the subject. Lull him into a sense of security and then spring her proposal on him. Always provided he didn't already have a wife. She sighed, wishing she knew more about Nick. Especially why he'd suddenly returned after all these years.

She flipped on her turn signal as she reached her destination and pulled into the farm's deeply rutted driveway.

A gasp escaped her as the car lurched from one gigantic pothole to another. Parking on a dirt patch in front of the house, she cut the engine and glanced around in disbelief. It had been years since she'd been here. But even so the changes were incredible.

The only similarity this derelict building had to the well-cared-for white farmhouse of her memory was its large-ness. Nothing else was even vaguely the same. Its white paint had blistered and peeled; half the windows on the ground floor were broken; the winter winds had torn quite a few of the shingles off the roof; some of the green shutters were entirely gone while others hung drunkenly on their hinges; and the long veranda across the front of the house, where she and Angie had spent many a summer afternoon dreaming of the magical days when they would be grown-up, was sagging.

When no one emerged from the house to see who had ar-rived, Jenny made her way across the swaying porch and knocked on the door.

The sound echoed eerily through the interior, but it brought no response. Reminding herself that Nora said Nick had been there earlier, Jenny walked around to the back. It looked just as bad as the front. The back porch railing had been pushed over, and waist-high weeds covered what had once been the yard. But someone had cut a path through them to the barn.

Had it been Nick? Excitement poured through her at this visible sign of his presence. Absently shifting the frozen pie from her left hand, which was beginning to go numb, to her right, she shaded her eyes against the bright sunlight and peered toward the barn about two hundred yards behind the house.

The same general air of decay and neglect hung over it, too. Had financial reverses driven Nick home? she specu-

lated. Surely, if he had any money, he wouldn't have allowed the farm to deteriorate to this extent. And if he didn't
have any capital, then perhaps, just perhaps, he'd be open
to a financial proposition. Hope began to grow in her.

She started toward the barn, instinctively hurrying as she
heard banging coming from inside. She slipped through the
half-open doors, blinking to adjust her vision to the dimly
lit interior. The single bulb dangling from a long cord
hanging from the rafters sent a faint pool of light over an
old truck. A man was leaning across the front fender, his
face hidden by the raised hood.

Jenny took a deep, steadying breath and moved closer,
her attention never wavering from him. He was wearing a
faded pair of snug jeans, scuffed Adidas and nothing else.
The skin on his bare back looked like well-polished teak,
smooth, unblemished and deeply tanned. She watched as
he did something to the engine and his formidable biceps
rippled from the effort.

Uneasily she measured the intimidating width of his
shoulders. Had Nick always been that muscular? She tried
to visualize the younger Nick of her memory, but all she
could remember with any degree of clarity were his eyes.
Bright blue eyes that had always been an effective barom-
eter of his mood. She could remember them darkening with
anger at one of her and Angie's pranks, but mostly they'd
gleamed with laughter and devilment. With the sheer joy
of being alive.

The nasty mutter that drifted out of the depths of the
truck's engine shook her free from her thoughts. She
watched as one large, grease-covered hand groped blindly
among the tools placed on the fender.

Correctly assuming that he was searching for the wrench
lying just beyond his reach, Jenny stepped forward and,
picking it up, pressed it into his hand.

"What the—" Nick jerked upright in surprise, smacking the back of his head against the hood. "Damn!" He shook his head to clear his vision.

Jenny stared uncertainly at him. It was Nick and yet it wasn't Nick. There was a subtle difference between the boy she remembered and the man she now faced. His hair was still a deep rich brown, only now the mahogany color was lightly threaded with gray. His face was still lean and roughly chiseled, but experience had carved deep lines in it. But it was his eyes that showed the greatest difference. Jenny shivered at their flat, hard surface. There was no expression whatsoever in their cold depths. But to her intense relief, even as she watched, a glimmer of annoyed humor lightened them.

"Of course, I should have known," he said ruefully. "My favorite redhead, little Jenny Ryton. No." His eyes narrowed as he noted the pie she was clutching to her chest like a shield. "Not so little anymore." A spark of something more elemental than humor darkened his eyes to blue gray as his attention focused on her breasts, stroking over the slight curves visible through the soft wool of her beige sweater. Slowly his gaze slipped lower, down over the swell of her abdomen to linger on the juncture of her thighs.

Jenny's breathing shortened as a strange fluttery feeling hit her stomach with the force of a blow. Disconcerted by a reaction that seemed totally divorced from rational thought, she instinctively took a step backward.

"Not little at all."

The amused thread sparkling through the deep velvet of his voice stiffened her wavering resolve. She wasn't some naive little eighteen-year-old with not the vaguest idea what was going on. She knew only too well what he was thinking. It was clearly written in the hot gleam in his eyes. What she wasn't so sure of was why she felt so threatened. Over the years she'd become highly adept at fielding much more blatant passes than his. If that's what his comment had been.

"You've improved almost past recognition," Nick said, wiping his hands on a dingy gray rag.

"It's been a long time," Jenny responded cautiously, her mouth drying as, unbidden, her eyes focused on the heavy coating of dark brown hair covering his broad chest.

"It has, at that." He wadded the cloth into a ball and flung it in the general direction of a wooden box in the corner. It missed.

"You never could hit the broad side of a barn," she inadvertently muttered her thoughts aloud.

"I was center on the high-school basketball team!" He was clearly outraged at what he saw as a slur on his abilities.

"Only because at six-four you were the tallest member on the team," she retorted.

"It takes talent to be six-four."

"Does not. It takes good genes." Her sense of disorientation was fading as she began catching glimpses of the old Nick buried in this harder, more mature version.

"Speaking of strange genes, what's that thing you're clutching like the crown jewels?"

"What?" She glanced down, becoming nervous again as she remembered her reason for calling. For a brief second her awareness of Nick as a man had overshadowed her concern for Jed, which only heightened her confusion.

"A cherry pie." She held it out to him. "A housewarming present."

"Thanks, but if it's to remain edible, you'd better keep it." He gestured with his oil-stained hands. "Would you take it into the kitchen for me?"

"Sure." Jenny eagerly grasped the opportunity. It would give her a chance to find out if he'd brought anyone with him. Such as a wife. It was going to be hard enough to work a proposal into the conversation. She had no intention of trying until she'd clarified his marital status.

Nick led the way back to the house, pushing open the back screen door, which had long since lost its netting, and motioning her inside.

"I put some coffee on earlier. Why don't you have a cup and tell me all about your husband," he suggested.

"Husband?" Jenny jerked around as his words uncannily echoed her thoughts and promptly tripped over the jagged doorsill.

Nick grabbed her, effortlessly pulling her against his broad chest to steady her.

Jenny tensed as her cheek brushed the polished warmth of his shoulder. The tangy smell of clean masculine sweat and the much more basic musky odor of the man himself flooded her nostrils, sending a shiver through her.

"Sorry." She hastily stepped back. "I'll just put the pie here on the table." She set it down, casting a surreptitious glance around the kitchen. It was in appalling shape. Chunks of plaster had been gouged out of the walls, litter was piled in the corners and mouse droppings were everywhere.

"Vandals." Nick's mouth tightened as he noticed her interest. "The sheriff ran them off, but not before they did quite a bit of damage."

"It's a shame," she sympathized.

"It's criminal, but fortunately, it's mostly surface stuff that I can easily fix."

"It must be hard on your wife." She tried to delicately probe.

"Unlike you, I've managed to resist the lure of matrimony. Here."

"Thanks." Jenny accepted the chipped mug of steaming coffee, keeping her eyes lowered to hide her growing excitement. So far, so good, she encouraged herself. "I'm not married, either," she corrected his false impression.

"You aren't?" A frown darkened his eyes. "I must have misunderstood. I thought Angie mentioned that you had a son."

"Jed." Jenny nodded. "But he's not my son. I mean, not legally. He's Tom and Cindi Foster's only child."

"Foster?" She watched with detached awe as he gulped the scalding brew. "Weren't they killed in a car accident a few years back?"

"Eight years ago. They were riding with someone who tried to beat a train to a crossing and didn't make it. Jed was a year old when his grandmother took him in."

"So how'd you get saddled with him?"

"By my own free will!" Jenny snapped. "He's a darling child."

"No nine-year-old kid is a darling," he said sardonically.

"Jed is, which you'd know if you met him," she stubbornly insisted. "Why don't you come to dinner tonight and judge for yourself? Then afterward—" she took a deep breath, gathering her courage "—afterward I have a proposition for you."

"A proposition!" He gave her a look of simulated horror. "Jenny Ryton!"

"A business proposition," she hastened to add. "I'm sure that a little extra money would come in handy with the plans that you have." She glanced significantly around the ravaged room, missing the arrested expression on his face.

"And the free meal would be nice, too," he said smoothly. "It *is* free, isn't it?"

"Of course it's free," she replied crossly, setting down her untouched coffee on the rickety table. "Since that's settled, I'll let you get back to your truck. We'll expect you about six?" She looked questioningly at him.

"Six is fine. Where are you living these days?"

"On Pulteney where Blanchard's Grocery used to be. I have a quilt shop on the ground floor. Jed and I live above it."

"A quilt shop," he mused. "I never knew you were interested in quilting."

"I don't imagine you ever really knew much about me," she observed without rancor. "As I remember, you used to think Angie and I were nothing but pests."

"You were," he muttered. "Remember the time the two of you ignored my warning and accepted a date with that pair of punks from Haverling?"

"But, Nick, they were the first older men who'd ever asked us out." Jenny laughed. "They must have been all of sixteen."

"To your thirteen. Your very immature thirteen."

"Well, we certainly didn't expect them to get drunk at the drive-in movies."

"Why not? They'd gotten drunk everywhere else."

"I will admit," she said reflectively, "Angie and I were never more glad in our lives to see you look in that car window."

"It happened to be at least the hundredth car window I'd looked in at that damn drive-in. I was petrified I'd get arrested as a Peeping Tom before I could locate the pair of you."

"I guess we did give you a few bad moments," she conceded, "but in all fairness that was twenty years ago. These days I'm a responsible, mature adult." *Who's out beating the bushes for a husband.* The incongruity of the thought made her squirm.

"Well, I'd best be off. I'll see you this evening." She gave him a bright, meaningless smile and retreated to her car, still puzzled over her reaction to Nick. She couldn't remember

the last time she'd responded to a man on such a purely sensual level. It was unlike her. Totally unlike her. So why was
it happening now? She worried the question around in her
mind. Maybe it was tied to the overall situation she found
herself in. It was certainly unsettling enough to account for
any aberration in her normal behavior, she thought wryly.
To suddenly find herself in the position of having to ask a
man to marry her went counter to every instinct she possessed. The mental effort involved in trying to carry it off
had tipped her off balance. That undoubtedly accounted for
a good part of her unexpected response. That and the fact
that he brought back memories of earlier, happier times. But
neither she nor Nick were the same people now. Then she'd
been a pesky adolescent to his fledgling adult. Now . . .

She frowned as she maneuvered her car down the rutted
driveway. Now they were meeting as equals, and it was
necessary to realign her whole way of thinking about him.
She sighed as she reached the road and accelerated. She
really didn't need another complication. She had enough
of them to deal with.

2

"JENNY? I'M HOME. Where are you?" Jed clattered up the back stairs, which rose from the shop's storeroom to the apartment.

"In the kitchen." Jenny glanced up, a warm, welcoming smile lighting her face as Jed burst into the room. She loved him so much. How could Social Services even consider taking him away? Panic washed through her. He was the center of her whole world.

Jed tossed his bulging book bag on the kitchen table and automatically opened the refrigerator, sticking his head inside.

"Don't hold the door open," Jenny just as automatically responded. "There're chocolate chip cookies in the jar."

Jed emerged from the depths of the refrigerator with a quart of milk and a carton of yogurt. "Can I have some of that instead?" He pointed to the three-layer cake Jenny was lavishly spreading chocolate fudge icing on.

"No, but I saved the icing bowl for you." She motioned to her right.

"What's the cake for?" Jed picked up a beater and began to industriously lick it clean.

"Dinner. We're having company." She squinted critically at the icing and decided it looked perfect.

"Jenny..." Jed paused, fidgeting with the dahlias in the bowl on the table. "What did Miss James say?"

"Miss James?" Jenny stalled. She'd hoped to get everything settled before she told Jed anything. There was no point in his worrying, too. She was already worried enough for both of them.

"She must have said something when she was here today."

"Why do you think Miss James was here?"

"Because when I came through the shop, I asked Mrs. . Norris if Miss James had finally come."

"And Marge said yes?" Jenny sighed.

"Not exactly. She said to ask you, which means that Miss James did come," he insisted. "Because otherwise she'd have said no."

"Excellent deductive reasoning." Jenny gave him a rueful smile.

"So what'd she say?" He tenaciously returned to the subject.

"Well . . ." Jenny made a production out of pouring him a glass of milk.

"What'd she say?" Jed's thin face looked pinched.

Jenny's heart twisted with pity. She had to tell him something. But what? For a second she considered the truth. That to get custody of him she needed a husband, and to get a husband she intended to sacrifice both her freedom and a large portion of her bank account. But she immediately thought better of the idea for several reasons. For one, Jed would never be able to resist sharing the information with his best friend, Bryan, who would undoubtedly tell a few other people until it became common knowledge. For another, it would poison any relationship between Jed and whomever she married, since the boy would be bound to feel that his new stepfather had taken advantage of the situation to get money out of her. But far more important, no nine-year-old should have to cope with the feelings of guilt that that kind of knowledge would bring.

No, she decided, the complete truth was out. She'd have to make do with part of it. Jed would undoubtedly have his suspicions when she married so opportunely, but as long as she didn't confirm them, that was all they'd be. Suspicions. And in time, if nothing happened to feed them, Jed would come to accept her marriage as one of those inexplicable adult impulses.

"Jed." She put her arms around him and drew him against her. It was a measure of how worried he was that he let her do it. Normally he had a fine contempt for hugging and kissing.

"Jed," she repeated helplessly, staring down into his soft gray eyes. "Miss James's first thought was that the Devlins can offer you a better home than I could."

"First thought?" Jed latched on to the phrase. "Does that mean she had a second thought?" He peered anxiously at Jenny, his thin body rigid with tension.

"She's going to think about it some more before she reaches a final decision. She's weighing the advantages that I can give you against those the Devlins can provide."

"What advantages?" he asked scathingly.

"For one thing, we don't have a father in our family, and Miss James feels that a growing boy needs a masculine role model." She tried to sound casual.

"Mr. Devlin!" Jed looked horrified. "He's a wimp! He doesn't know anything about baseball or football or hockey or lacrosse or..." He sputtered to an indignant stop. "All he ever does is read soppy poetry!" His voice held a wealth of scorn.

"That's as may be, but there's lots of different types of men, my lad," Jenny felt obliged to point out. "Masculinity can't be measured by a liking for blood sports."

"Baseball isn't a blood sport."

"It is the way you play it." She gently ruffled his silky black hair.

"Jenny, if Miss James is worried about . . ." He paused pensively, studying the fancy cake. "We're having company for dinner? A man?"

"Yes. Nick Carlton. His sister was my best friend all through school."

"Jenny?" He gave her an adult look. "Are you going to get me a dad so we'll be like the Devlins?"

As she had feared, Jed immediately made the connection between her invitation to Nick and her problems with getting custody of him. Quickly she moved to alleviate his suspicions.

"A husband for me would certainly be a point in our favor, but unfortunately, despite the fact that Nick's hinted at marriage, he's never actually asked me," she told him, blending a plausible lie with the truth.

Jed frowned. "I never met any Nick Carlton."

"He's been in the Middle East for years."

"Then how could he have hinted at marriage?" he asked, skeptical.

"Letters. We've always corresponded, and now he's back home. It was good to see him again," she threw in for good measure.

"When did you see him!"

Jenny was hard-pressed to keep from laughing at Jed's indignant expression. He sounded exactly like an irate father.

"This afternoon when I invited him to dinner."

"You know, Jenny, I have a much better idea than this Nick."

"Oh?" Her voice was apprehensive. Jed's ideas had an uncanny way of getting out of hand.

"It's simple logic, really." He beamed at her. "We're at a disadvantage with the Devlins because we don't have a dad in our family, right?"

"Right."

"Well, while getting a husband for you would make us equals, the same thing could be accomplished by getting rid of Mr. Devlin."

"Getting rid of Mr. Devlin?" she repeated. "I rather think that's beyond my powers."

"Of course it is," Jed scoffed. "You can't even squash the slugs in the garden. We'll simply have to find us a hit man."

"What!" Jenny stared at him in horror.

"A hit man. Gramma says that it always pays to go to a specialist."

"Your grandmother was talking about doctors and where did you hear about hit men?"

"On TV." He looked surprised at her question.

"But we never—"

"Not here. At Bryan's. His folks have a VCR, and his dad rents these really great movies from the drugstore."

"Oh, Lord." Jenny rubbed her forehead. Just what she needed. One more thing to worry about.

"Listen, Jed, no more TV at Bryan's, and I mean it."

"Ah, Jenny..."

"And to get back to your original idea, think how poor Mrs. Devlin would feel if someone were to shoot her husband."

Jed frowned, obviously giving it serious thought. "I don't think she'd mind if he didn't bleed on her carpet," he finally decided.

Jenny opened her mouth and then closed it when she found that she had nothing to say. She had the sneaking suspicion there was a germ of truth in his assessment of Mrs. Devlin's reaction.

"Well, moral considerations aside, hit men are rather hard to come by in a small town like Litton." She concentrated on the one aspect of the situation he might understand.

"I could ask around," he offered.

"You could go pick some peas for dinner," she said quellingly. "I want this evening to be a success."

UNFORTUNATELY, IT WAS a wish that was doomed from the moment Jed answered the front door and found himself confronted by six feet four inches of overwhelming masculinity. It took only one glance for the boy to realize that Nick Carlton was quite a different proposition from the usual run of Jenny's male acquaintances. As young as Jed was, he immediately recognized the authority and strength of purpose emanating from the man. Recognized it and instinctively began resisting.

Jed frowned at Nick's open-necked knit shirt and launched his opening salvo. "Why aren't you wearing a tie?"

"I don't like them." Nick stepped around the boy and into the small living room. "Where's Jenny?"

"Helping a late customer in the shop. She said to tell you to make yourself at home. That she'll be back in a minute."

Nick sat down on the sofa and speculatively studied Jed's belligerent expression. Perhaps the kid was simply nervous in his role as substitute host, Nick thought, giving Jed the benefit of the doubt.

"Jenny said I was to offer you a drink." Jed gestured toward the cabinet behind him.

"Thank you." Nick got to his feet, and Jed instinctively retreated. Nick pretended not to notice as he fixed himself a large Scotch and soda and added a couple of ice cubes from the container beside the liquor. Suppressing a sigh, he sat back down under Jed's disapproving stare.

"Do you always drink so much?"

"Always, but I'm not dangerous until after the third drink. Unless provoked," he added smoothly.

Jed blinked nervously and squared his thin shoulders. "Jenny's my mother."

"She mentioned that."

"When?" Jed shot the question at him.

"When she was out to the farm this afternoon." Nick kept his irritation at being cross-examined out of his voice with an effort. "Jenny and I go way back."

"She can't like you that much if she never mentioned you to me before today."

"Did she ever mention that you should be polite to guests?" Nick asked mildly, wondering what was going on. The kid clearly disliked him and it made no sense. Unless he was completely antisocial, which Nick very much doubted.

"You aren't my guest!" Jed glared at him. "I—" He broke off as the back door opened and Jenny hurried in.

"Hi, Nick. Sorry not to be here when you arrived, but..." Her welcoming smile faltered slightly as the tense atmosphere in the living room engulfed her. She glanced from Nick's impassive face to Jed's set expression, trying to make sense of the vibrations she was getting. The sound of the timer in the kitchen distracted her and with a muttered "Excuse me" she rushed to turn the oven off before the biscuits were scorched. She wanted this evening to be a success. So much depended on it.

But despite the tender perfection of the fried chicken smothered in cream gravy, the fluffy mashed potatoes, the fresh peas and the homemade biscuits, the atmosphere at the dinner table grew progressively more strained.

Mostly her own fault, Jenny admitted as she nervously rearranged the food on her plate. She should have foreseen that Jed might be jealous of a strange man who suddenly appeared on the scene. Especially a man she claimed to know quite well. Gamely she took a fortifying gulp of her wine and broke the oppressive silence.

"Did you ever get the truck working, Nick?" she asked.

"Not yet."

"It pays to hire specialists to take care of things." Jed gave Jenny a significant stare.

"Jed!" She turned to him in exasperation.

"Yes, Jenny?" He gave her an angelic smile. "What did—"

The shrill beeping of a car horn interrupted him.

Jenny frowned, hurrying across the tiny dining room to peer down into the street below.

"It's the Pearsons' car. Why would... Good Lord, it's Thursday night. I forgot all about your Cub Scout meeting. Hurry up, Jed. Don't keep them waiting."

"I can't go to Cub Scouts," he protested. "Not with..." He cast a furtive glance at Nick, who smiled blandly back at him.

"Jed, that's enough!" she snapped. "You'll go to your meeting the way you do every Thursday night, and you'll go this instant."

"Yes, Jenny." He seemed to realize that he'd pushed her too far.

"Don't forget your jacket, and I'll pick you boys up at the usual time," she called after him as he clattered down the front stairs.

"Okay," his voice drifted back.

Jenny waited by the window until he'd emerged from the house. Her breath escaped on a relieved sigh as he climbed into the Pearsons' yellow station wagon. Now she could talk without having to worry that Jed might overhear.

She turned back to Nick to find him watching her intently.

"Would you like a cup of coffee?" she murmured. Now that the moment was actually upon her, she was uncertain of how to actually broach the subject uppermost in her mind.

"Later." Nick rose from the table and walked over to her. "You've been as nervous as a kitten all evening." He eyed her thoughtfully. "And you weren't all that calm this afternoon. What is it about me that seems to put you on edge, Jenny?" He reached out and ran his knuckles over her flushed cheek.

Jenny sucked in her breath as pinpricks of static electricity danced over her skin. Hastily she backed up a step and briefly closed her eyes, trying to get a firm grip on her skittering emotions. She cleared her throat and decided on a forthright approach. Her nerves would never last through a long-drawn-out appeal.

"It isn't you, Nick. At least, not you exactly," she elaborated, noticing his skeptical look.

"Isn't it?" He sank down on the sofa. "I feel like the specter at the feast, what with that kid glaring at me as if I were about to foreclose on the old homestead and you jumping like a scalded cat every time I come near."

"Forget Jed for the moment," Jenny said.

"Personally, I'd just as soon forget him permanently."

Jenny sighed, not really blaming Nick. Jed's behavior this evening hadn't exactly been calculated to win friends and influence people.

"Nick?" Jenny sat down beside him and turned to face him. "I said earlier that I had a financial proposition for you." She glanced down at her hands, surprised to see them clenched into fists.

"I don't remember you ever having trouble expressing yourself before." His large hand closed encouragingly over hers, and Jenny shivered as his callused palm scraped across her soft skin. The sensation echoed through her, scattering her hard-won self-possession.

"As a matter of fact," he continued, "as I recall, I never could get you and Angie to shut up. Suppose you simply spit it out. What do you want?"

"To marry you!" she blurted out, flinching as his hand suddenly closed over hers with bruising force. "I mean, not you in particular," she tried to explain in the face of his incredulous expression. "Any man would do. It's nothing personal," she babbled.

"Is that supposed to make me feel better?" He released her hands and stood, glaring down at her.

Jenny's heart sank as she realized she'd just blown it. Nick was angry. No, furious. She watched the tiny sparks exploding in his bright blue eyes.

"Tell me—" his voice was heavy with irony "—for what do you need this husband that anyone will do?"

"For Jed," she said starkly. "I want him."

He frowned at her. "You already have him."

"Not legally." She sighed despondently.

"Exactly how did you get involved with the kid?" Nick perched on the edge of the chair across from her.

Of their own volition, her eyes were drawn to the way the thin fabric of his beige pants stretched tautly over his muscled thigh as his long leg swung back and forth. Horrified at the direction her thoughts were taking, she forced herself to focus on his question.

"I first met Jed when he was about three. His grandmother was a good customer of mine, and she brought him into the shop one day. It was obvious that he was too much for her. Her health simply wasn't up to taking care of an active child. At first I offered to take him out for a day because I liked his grandmother and wanted to give her a rest. But as I got to know Jed, I began to take him out because I liked him for himself. Soon he was spending an occasional night, then weekends, until finally, when his grandmother went into the hospital four and a half years ago for hip-replacement surgery, Jed moved in with me and simply stayed. It's worked out very well. Jed had me, I had him and his grandmother was able to enjoy him without the stress of trying to raise him."

"So what happened to upset this idealistic state of affairs?"

"His grandmother's health has made it necessary for her to go into a nursing home. When the social worker at the home was doing the paperwork, she discovered Jed's irregular living arrangements. The home reported it to Social Services, which decided 'steps must be taken.'" She bitterly quoted the letter she'd received.

"So you applied to adopt him?" Nick prodded when she fell silent.

"Yes. In my stupidity I assumed that since I'd had him for more than four years, it would simply be a matter of filling out the paperwork."

"I take it it wasn't?"

"Social Services feels that Jed needs a male role model."

"The kid certainly needs something," Nick muttered.

Ignoring his unpromising comment, she continued, "If I can come up with a husband, I can have him. If I can't, he goes elsewhere." Her voice broke.

"So you hatched this harebrained scheme?" he scoffed. "Why haven't you already got a husband? Are you still grieving for David?"

"No," she said slowly. "I'm not. Oh, I still wish he hadn't been killed in Vietnam, but the grief has passed. All that's left is regret for the waste of his life and for what might have been."

"Then why haven't you ever married?" he persisted.

"It takes two to marry, my friend," she said tartly. "I didn't recover from David's death overnight. I was twenty-two when he died. It wasn't until almost two years later that I felt like getting on with my life. But by that time the majority of the men I knew were either married or had left the area in search of better jobs. Like you did. All that were left were men who were unmarried for very good reasons."

"I see," Nick said slowly.

Taking heart that his earlier fury seemed to have faded somewhat, Jenny decided to press her offer.

"I'm not suggesting that you tie yourself to Jed and me forever, Nick. The adoption becomes final in a year, and then we can get an amicable divorce. You can go your own way seventy-five thousand richer."

"Seventy-five thousand?"

"I'm not asking you to do this out of the goodness of your heart. I invested the proceeds from the sale of my grandfather's farm when I inherited it six years ago. My stock portfolio is worth about a hundred and fifty thousand now. You can have half as a payment for a year of your time, and the rest will ensure Jed's education no matter what happens to me."

Nick frowned into her tense face. "Are you sure the kid's worth what you're doing for him?"

"Don't judge him by tonight's performance, Nick. He's as worried as I am about what might happen, and he's reacting by being a bit of a brat. But I love him, bad behavior and all. Can't you see that?" she pleaded.

"Yes, I see." A rueful smile curved his lean lips. "I once had a puppy who was as ugly as sin and had the manners of a pig, but to me he was perfect."

"Will you marry me?" Jenny repeated, encouraged by the softened expression on his face.

Nick gave her a long speculative look. "What are you going to do if I refuse?"

"Make a list of unattached males I know and start proposing. Surely someone out there needs seventy-five thousand."

"Dammit, woman!" he exploded. "Of all the stupid ideas! You just got through telling me that the unattached men you know aren't married for good reason."

"I'd marry the devil himself if it meant I could keep Jed," she said flatly.

"Hell!" Nick ran his fingers through his thick brown hair.

"Won't you at least consider my proposition?" Jenny abandoned the last remnants of her pride and tried plain begging.

"I wonder if you have any idea of just what you're asking," Nick murmured absently. "Or, more precisely, what you're asking for. I'll think about it, Jenny."

He headed toward the front door. "But in exchange I want your word that you won't approach any other unsuspecting male in the meantime."

"All right." Jenny nodded, wondering if his agreeing to consider her proposal was an encouraging sign. He certainly hadn't embraced her idea with open arms, but on the other hand, he hadn't turned her down flat, either.

By Saturday morning she was beginning to wish that he had. Even a negative reply would have been better than the churning uncertainty that gripped her every time the phone rang or the door of her shop opened. At least if he'd refused, she could have begun to make secondary plans. As it was, she felt suspended in limbo. Trapped in a situation over which she had absolutely no control.

The muted ringing of the phone interrupted her conversation with a customer, and with an apologetic smile she turned to answer it, breathing a silent prayer that it would be Nick. Preferably Nick with good news.

It wasn't. Her stomach twisted as she recognized the clear, ringing tones of Miss James.

"I've been waiting for your call, Miss Ryton." There was the faintest hint of reproach in her voice.

"I'm so sorry not to have called, Miss James, but..." Jenny glanced around the shop, seeking an inspiration. It came as her gaze alighted on a battered shopping bag a customer was carrying emblazoned with the motto Visit St. John Island, Jewel of the West Indies. "I haven't been able to reach my parents," she improvised. "It seems that they went on a weekend trip with their local senior citizens' group. Their neighbor said they'd be home Sunday night, so I should be able to get back to you on Monday."

"Don't bother to call," Miss James said. "Simply bring him by. I'll be in my office anytime between ten and noon."

"Bring him by?" Jenny repeated blankly.

"We can hardly okay an adoption without meeting the father-to-be," Miss James said impatiently. "Although I'm certain in your case it's simply a formality. Anyone you would consider marrying is bound to be an acceptable father."

"Jed is very fond of him." Jenny perjured her soul without a qualm. "We'll see you on Monday, then." She hastily brought the conversation to a close before Miss James asked any leading questions. Such as the name of her mythical husband-to-be.

Jenny hung up the phone with fingers that shook. She could almost feel the net closing over her. In two days she was going to have to produce a fiancé. If Nick weren't willing... Deliberately she blanked the possibility from her mind. He had to be willing. He simply had to be because if he wasn't... A grim smile twisted her soft lips as a picture of her knocking on every door in town and asking if there was an unattached male inside who was willing to marry her filled her mind.

"Trouble?" Marge asked.

"Maybe. Listen, Marge—" Jenny glanced up at the clock "—could you and Letty hold the fort for a while? I need to see someone. I'll be back by noon."

"Of course we can. Don't worry about the shop," Marge said soothingly. "Take all the time you need."

"Thanks." Jenny gave her a grateful smile. She felt guilty leaving Marge to cope with the brisk Saturday-morning trade with only a teenager for help, but it was vital that she see Nick.

Jenny spent the short trip out to the farm trying to think of an approach she could use that would balance the necessity of getting an immediate answer from Nick against the danger of making him feel pressured. To her relief the battered car he'd borrowed from his cousin Liz was parked in front of the house. At least she wasn't going to have to chase all over town trying to find him. She parked her Caravan and switched off the engine.

"Get on with it," she ordered herself. "You don't have time to dither."

Determinedly she marched around the house and pounded on the back door. There was no answer. Opening the door, she stuck her head inside. The kitchen was empty. Empty not only of Nick, but also of the litter that had filled the room the last time she'd been there. It was not much of an improvement. Without the cloaking cover of the trash, the room's generally deteriorated condition was even more obvious. It was going to take a great deal of time and money to get this room into any kind of shape. The knowledge encouraged her. Closing the dilapidated screen door behind her, she headed toward the barn.

Its doors hung open to allow the brilliant September sunshine to lighten the gloomy interior. Purposefully she stepped inside. A feeling of déjà vu engulfed her as she caught sight of Nick's muscular torso bent over the engine of the old truck. Taking a deep breath, she crossed the littered concrete floor.

"Nick?" The word came out in a hoarse croak that dismayed her. She wanted to sound sure of herself, even if she wasn't. She cleared her throat and tried again. "Nick, I want to talk to you."

"I rather figured that." He emerged from the engine's depths and, setting down a greasy piece of metal, turned to her.

It was all Jenny could do to prevent herself from retreating as the sheer raw force of his potent masculinity reached out to engulf her. Her gaze traced the broad width of his chest, becoming entangled in the thick pelt of chocolate-brown hair that covered it. Compulsively her regard slipped downward past where the hair disappeared into the waistband of his snug jeans, down over his flat stomach to linger on the unmistakable masculine shape of his thighs.

"I think I'd better wash this off." He glanced ruefully at the oil dripping off his hands.

"Wash?" Jenny latched on to the prosaic word.

"Hmm, up at the house. Then we'll have that talk you're so keen on."

She hurried along beside him, dreading the coming interview.

He shouldered open the kitchen door and motioned her inside.

Jenny slipped through. A spark of awareness darted across her skin as her bare arm brushed his muscular forearm. She dropped onto the room's one chair while he flipped on the water with his elbow and began to lather his hands. She watched with an absorbed interest as the muscles in his sleek back rippled with his movements. He really was in superb physical shape, she realized. He was all muscle. There wasn't an ounce of fat anywhere on him. What had he been doing all those years since he'd left Litton? He certainly hadn't had a desk job. Both his well-developed body and his deep tan suggested some sort of outdoor work. She searched her memory for some tidbit of information that Angie might have included in her letters, but nothing came to mind.

"You were saying?" Nick's brisk voice interrupted her speculations, and she hastily turned to him. He was leaning against the battered kitchen counter, his arms folded across his broad chest, the picture of indolent ease.

He had no right to look so calm, she thought sourly. Not when she felt as if she were about to shatter at any moment into a million pieces.

"I'm sorry to track you down, but when you didn't call..." She paused to give him a chance to explain his silence. When he didn't, she was forced to continue. "I simply don't have the luxury of waiting indefinitely, Nick. The caseworker called today. She wants to meet my intended, whomever that might be."

"Meet him?"

"More accurately, give him the once-over. You know, make sure he's of sound mind and morals. You are, aren't you?" A horrible thought struck her. Twenty years was a long time. Who knew what he might have done?

"Don't worry," he said dryly. "I've never been caught with my hand in the cookie jar."

Never been caught. The words echoed in her mind. Did that mean he'd never done anything wrong or merely that he'd never been *caught* doing anything wrong? She eyed him uneasily. There was a big difference.

"Now what are you imagining, Jenny Ryton?" Nick asked softly. "Your eyes are as big as saucers. You missed your calling. You should have taken up writing."

"What I want to take up is motherhood." She determinedly pushed her doubts to the back of her mind. She couldn't afford to be squeamish at this stage.

"You haven't changed your mind?" He frowned at her.

"Changed my mind!" she said with a gasp. "We're not talking about a carpet I want to buy. We're talking about a living, breathing human being. Moreover, one I consider my son. I told you, whatever it takes to keep him, I'll do it."

"Dammit, Jenny! You're supposed to be a levelheaded businesswoman—"

"Thank you, but even levelheaded businesswomen have children they love."

"You always were a stubborn little cuss." He rubbed the back of his neck in exasperation. "Can't you see that what you're proposing is a one-way ticket to disaster?"

"All I can see is that I'm going to lose Jed if I don't go through with it. Nick, we've been over all this. It doesn't have to be a disaster. It can work out very well for everyone concerned. All it takes is one year for the adoption to become final. One year and I'll have Jed and you'll have sufficient funds to at least make a start on modernizing your farm. Or to do anything else you want. If you're worried about my trying to pull a fast one on you, I'll give you the money the day we're married."

"I'm not the least bit worried about you, or anyone else for that matter, trying to cheat me." His face settled into hard lines that sent a shiver of apprehension through her. An apprehension she tried to tell herself was ridiculous. This was Nick Carlton. She'd known him all her life. But she'd known the boy and this was the man, the unsettling thought surfaced.

"I have to do this, Nick," she pleaded. "Why can't you see that?"

"Oh, I can see. The question is, can you?"

"What?" She blinked, uncertain of what he was getting at.

"Come here." His softly growled order tugged her to her feet. "I want to check something."

"What? My teeth are all my own," she quipped.

"And is everything your own?" he asked as his eyes dropped suggestively to her small breasts, clearly outlined under the thin cotton of her green blouse.

"Certainly." She stood her ground. She wasn't going to allow herself to be flustered by the unmistakable signs of sexual passion quickening to life in his eyes. She was a mature woman, well able to parry sexual teasing, she reminded herself.

"Just a little closer, Jenny," his dark voice urged.

She found herself automatically responding, moving forward until she was standing directly in front of him, her face inches from his bare chest.

Her nose twitched as the musky scent of his sun-warmed skin filtered into her nostrils, charging the air in her lungs. The heat from his body rushed out to envelop her, seeming to isolate the two of them in a world of their own. Her fingertips began to tingle as they imagined the crispness of the cloud of curling hair. Clenching her hands into fists to dispel the feeling, she looked up into Nick's face. His features had hardened into sharp planes and angles, and the gleam in his eyes had become a devouring flame.

She moistened her dry lips and tried to lighten the atmosphere. "What are we doing?"

"I sincerely hope that's a rhetorical question." He gave her a slow, sensual smile. "Or this is going to be a lot more difficult than I anticipated."

"I was simply trying—"

"You don't have to try. You always were an aggravating little devil. Always getting into trouble that I had to bail you out of. You haven't changed a bit."

"I am not always in trouble. Believe me, I've had a very uneventful life up till now."

"No boyfriends around?" He shot her a penetrating glance.

"Use your head!" she snapped. "If I had a boyfriend, I wouldn't have had to approach you."

"That rather depends," he replied, unmoved by her anger. "He could be ineligible for marriage." His large hands cupped her soft hips, and Jenny instinctively jumped, colliding with his chest. It was like bumping into a wall. There was no give. She could feel the soft fullness of her breasts crushed against him.

Tentatively she wiggled, trying to gain a little breathing space, but he didn't seem to notice her efforts and she was loath to react like an outraged spinster. After all, he wasn't hurting her or even frightening her. What he was doing was making her extremely aware of him as a sensual being. It was not a feeling she welcomed.

"Ineligible?" She tried to use words to drive some space between them.

"As in married."

"Married?" The word jarred.

"Mmm. Married men have been known to fool around."

"Not with me they haven't," she said flatly. "Even if I didn't have Jed to consider, I'd never engage in a casual affair with a married man. I don't have a masochistic bone in my body."

"I have a feeling that no affair you indulged in would ever be casual." His gaze fastened on her lips, and to her dismay she could feel them start to tingle.

"Don't—" she began, only to have her words swallowed as his mouth closed over hers. He lifted her, arching her lower body into his. Automatically her hands clutched his shoulders for support.

A small moan escaped as his tongue slipped between her teeth and began a thorough exploration of the moist warmth inside. She shuddered at the onslaught of sensation that shook her at the escalating intimacy of his kiss. She could feel the hardening force of his manhood against her soft thighs, a development that did nothing for her reeling composure.

Finally he raised his head and stared down at her.

Jenny stepped back, faintly surprised that her trembling legs could still support her. Determinedly she held her ground, when every instinct she possessed was screaming at her to escape while she still could.

"Nick, why are you confusing the issue with sex?"

"I was *clarifying* the issue with sex," he said. "I wanted to know what it would be like to kiss you."

"Oh?" Jenny muttered, curious to know what he'd thought but too cautious to ask.

"Exactly what kind of marriage are you offering me, Jenny?"

"I told you, seventy-five thousand for a year of your time."

He shook his head. "I'm not talking about money. I'm talking about the physical side of things. I want it clearly understood exactly what the parameters of this marriage are before the vows."

"Understood?" she repeated weakly, knowing precisely what he was getting at, but not wanting to face it. If that kiss was anything to go by, Nick Carlton was not only a highly sensual man, but also a very experienced one.

"To put it bluntly, if I marry you, I'll expect to share your bed."

"Does that mean you'll do it?" Hope flared to life at his words. The rest she ignored. She'd examine her headlong reaction to his kiss later in private.

There was an infinitesimal pause before he said, "If you're sure it's what you want. But only on my terms."

"Agreed." She barely heard the caveat. She was too excited. She'd done it! Jed was hers. She hurried to the door, anxious to get home and share the news of her impending marriage with Jed. "I'll call you tomorrow to make plans." She threw the words over her shoulder as she left.

"You fool," Nick castigated himself. "Did you really think you'd scare her off with a kiss?"

He was the one who should be scared, he thought ruefully. He'd intended to use that kiss to frighten her into facing what could happen if she insisted on marrying a man she didn't know all that well. He'd planned to use his superior strength to graphically demonstrate her vulnerability. To inexorably drive home the point that, since her marriage had to last a year, she would have to deal with the appetites of her husband, and she had no idea what they might be.

But it hadn't worked out that way. He wasn't quite sure why, but he'd lost sight of his purpose the minute he'd taken her in his arms. All he'd been able to think about was the feel of her soft breasts pressed against his bare chest, the impact of her slender fingers digging into the muscles of his shoulders and the incredibly sweet taste of her mouth.

But there was more to his agreeing to marry her than just an unexpectedly explosive sexual encounter, he thought, trying to analyze the reason for his capitulation. The threads that bound him to Jenny had been forged in his boyhood. Looking out for her and Angie was a deeply ingrained habit that, when it came right down to it, he was strangely reluctant to break.

A muted buzzing interrupted his thoughts, and he walked into the living room and picked up the mobile phone lying on the neatly made camp cot.

"Carlton here."

"Good morning, Nick," a slightly accented voice greeted him. "It's Murad. I have news."

"Good or bad?" Mentally he braced himself.

"I'd categorize it as cautiously optimistic," Murad hedged. "After the way you helped my father deal with the radical elements in Abar when he inherited the throne, he feels he owes you. So he's agreed to most of Witton's kidnappers' demands."

"Most?"

"He's willing to free forty-eight of the fifty jailed men the terrorists are demanding in exchange for your colleague."

"If he's willing to release forty-eight, why not the last two?"

"Because the days of absolute monarchies are over, my friend. Even here in Abar," Murad said dryly. "The two he won't release were convicted last year of bombing an elementary school. Releasing them would have horrendous political repercussions."

"Probably. Still, getting forty-eight men for Witton isn't a bad return on their investment. If we just knew a little more about his kidnappers . . ." he said in frustration.

"I'm working on it, Nick, but getting any solid information isn't easy. This particular group of terrorists seems to have sprung up out of nowhere. The only thing we know for certain about them is what you managed to find out last spring."

"I wish to God I'd stayed out of it. If I had, Don wouldn't be a hostage with a threat of execution hanging over him."

"You're allowing your emotions to intrude on your common sense, Nick," Murad chided. "If murder had been the terrorists' objective, they'd have killed him on the spot. No, they've clearly decided that Witton is worth more to them alive than dead. So we'll bargain with them."

"At least we've something to bargain with. Thank your father for his cooperation, would you, Murad?"

"Sure, and would you pass on these latest developments to Witton's wife? Try to sound optimistic without being specific because I haven't the vaguest idea of what kind of time frame we're talking about. I'll have to haggle a bit with them because if I don't, they'll think we're a weak touch and simply up the ante."

"Probably, but do your best to speed it up, Murad. I'm worried about Adelaide's ability to hold up under pressure."

"Anything I can do to help?"

"Just what you are. She won't accept anything else," Nick said in frustration. "She wouldn't let me stay with her in New York City because she said she couldn't pretend that it hadn't happened if she saw me every time she turned around. She wouldn't even let me move her into a hotel where she'd at least have some people around her. She said Don told her to wait at the apartment until he returned to the States, and that's exactly what she intends to do."

"Women," Murad groaned. "They're irrational at the best of times, let alone when they're pregnant. Well, we'll do our best to make sure Witton is released before the baby comes in November."

"Don will be home to see his child born, no matter what it takes. I promised Adelaide," he said harshly.

"Nick!" Murad snapped. "Don't you dare do something stupid like flying back here. You know you're the one that group really wants. Once they get their hands on you, it won't be a matter of bargaining for your life, but for your body. They want to kill you in the worst way, and I *do* mean the worst way. You promised you'd let me handle this."

"No, I promised I'd let you *try* to handle it. If you can't—"

"I can," Murad gritted out. "I just told you, my father's given me plenty to bargain with. Just make sure that you don't blow everything by coming back here."

"For the present you have a completely free hand," Nick assured him.

"Thanks, I'm going to hold you to it. Take care. I'll keep you informed."

"Bye." Thoughtfully Nick hung up. For the first time since the kidnapping he allowed himself to hope that Murad would be able to successfully negotiate Don's release.

3

"BUT, JENNY, I don't want to ride to the wedding with Mrs. Norris!" Jed wailed. "I want to go with you." Angrily he turned off the Saturday cartoons.

"Thanks a lot, bub." Marge winced as she wiggled her toes in her tight new shoes. "That's the story of my life. All my escorts prefer another woman. Although in this case, I can't say that I blame you." Marge eyed Jenny's cream wool suit approvingly. "You look gorgeous, Jenny. Not precisely bridal, but very elegant."

"She looks like my mother," Jed protested.

Jenny sighed at the belligerent expression on Jed's face. All those magazine articles that said children found it hard to accept a stepparent were right. Jed's dislike of Nick had not softened at all in the week since she'd told him that they intended to marry. She hoped that once Jed became better acquainted with Nick, he'd begin to see him as a person instead of merely as a potential rival for Jenny's affection.

"Please go with Marge, Jed." Jenny straightened his tie and gently brushed a wayward strand of inky-black hair out of his eyes. "It's getting late." She glanced at the clock on the television. Nick would be here in a few minutes, and she didn't want any witnesses when she told him of the change of venue for their wedding. Maybe he wouldn't mind, she encouraged herself, knowing it was a forlorn hope. She minded herself, minded terribly, so she could hardly expect him to like it any better.

"Come on, Jed." Marge captured his hand and started toward the front stairs.

"Would you stick your head in the shop and make sure Letty knows where the order form for that salesman from VIP is in case he stops by, Marge? I meant to tell her, but I can't remember if I actually did."

"That's because the human brain can't tell the difference between thinking you're going to do something and actually doing it," Jed told her.

"Is that so?" Marge grinned. "And here I thought it was just a sign of getting old. You can tell me all about it on the way." Marge hustled him out.

The echo of their footsteps on the stairs had barely died away before she heard Nick coming up them. Jenny turned toward the door as he entered.

She blinked, staring at the exquisitely tailored perfection of his three-piece gray suit, her eyes lingering on the somber magnificence of his navy silk tie. Where had he acquired such an obviously expensive outfit and why? What kind of job had he had that required such a wardrobe? Or perhaps it was simply a case of his preferring to invest in one good suit as opposed to buying several cheap ones? And Nick had been living in the Middle East, she reminded herself. Tailors there were probably very reasonable.

"I passed Mrs. Norris and the kid outside the shop. She said you were waiting to talk to me?" His voice cut short her speculations.

"Yes, there's been a slight change in plans."

"If you're trying to tell me the wedding's been postponed, forget it. I'm not getting dressed up again."

"No, that's not the problem. Although you ought to wear a suit more often. It makes you look very. . ." She paused, trying to analyze the impression she was getting. It was as if he'd not only donned a new suit, but a new aura to go with it. He seemed to radiate authority.

"Try impatient!" He glanced at the wafer-thin watch on his wrist. "We're due at the justice of the peace in ten minutes."

"We aren't being married by the justice of the peace," she blurted out. "We're being married by Reverend Marston in the Methodist church."

"Oh?" His blue eyes narrowed as they studied her flushed face. "And why did you change our plans without first consulting me?"

"Because you weren't there to consult. I've been trying to reach you every day since we got that blasted license, but the farm's been deserted and I could hardly run around town asking if anyone had seen my fiancé!"

"I was in New York City," he bit out. "I wasn't aware that this agreement of ours included getting my travel plans approved."

"I'm sorry," she said, knowing he had a valid point. "I didn't mean to imply that." She walked over to the coffee table and picked up her cream leather gloves. She pulled them on, meticulously smoothing out the wrinkles as if the very normalcy of her actions could somehow normalize the situation between them.

"Poor Jenny." Nick's voice came from right behind her and she jumped. For such a large man he moved like a cat. "You're a bundle of nerves, and my snapping at you isn't helping any." His hands settled on her shoulders, and he eased her back against the hard wall of his chest. The tang of his cologne drifted into her lungs, and the heat from his body penetrated the fine wool of her suit, seeping into her tense muscles.

"Relax. That's right," he murmured encouragingly as her body, with a will of its own, obeyed.

Just this once she'd lean on someone, she thought. She was so tired of coping with everything on her own.

"Now, breathe deeply." His voice had a hypnotic quality to it. "In, out. That's right. Take it easy. You said this wedding was what you wanted. Remember, Jenny?"

"Yes." She firmed her rubbery muscles and stepped away from him. "It's what has to be."

"Now suppose you tell me why we're being married in the church?"

"Because at heart I'm a chicken," she admitted ruefully. "It seems that Mrs. Luftus's niece works in the county offices, and she told her aunt that we'd gotten a wedding license who told Nora Fleming who told—"

"The whole town," he said in resignation. "It's nice to know that some things don't change."

"That's one way of looking at it." Jenny chuckled. "Anyway, on Tuesday Reverend Marston came into the shop and wanted to know when we'd be needing the church for the wedding. I tried to tell him that we were just going to have a quick ceremony because of Jed's custody case, but he began reminiscing about when he married your parents in a big hurry because your father was being shipped out during World War Two. And then he went on to tell me about how one of the bridesmaids fainted halfway up the aisle when he married my folks and how you bit him when he christened you." An inadvertent giggle escaped her.

"Slander." Nick grinned.

"And then when he smiled at me and said how much he was looking forward to marrying us—" she shrugged "—I just didn't have the heart to tell him we were going to a justice of the peace, Nick. And it doesn't really make any difference where we're married."

"I suppose not, but if we don't hurry, we aren't going to get married anywhere." He took her arm and started toward the door.

Jenny sped along beside him, too relieved that he was taking it so well to complain that she was having to trot to keep up with his long-legged stride.

She blinked as they emerged into the afternoon sunlight and then blinked again as she saw the car he was steering her toward. It was a brand-new, bright red Corvette.

"Like it?" He opened the door and helped her in.

Jenny leaned back against the cream leather seat and studied the complicated-looking dashboard.

"It's certainly . . . impressive." To say nothing of expensive, she thought. The seventy-five thousand she was going to give him wouldn't last long if he bought many playthings like this. That must have been why he'd gone to New York, she suddenly realized. To buy this metal monstrosity. All Litton boasted was a small Ford dealership.

"I always wanted a Corvette." He reverently turned the ignition key, and the engine instantly throbbed to life. "Buckle your seat belt."

"I hope I'm not going to need it," she muttered, shoving the buckle into the lock. "The speed limit between here and the church is only twenty-five."

"And I hope you're not going to turn into a nagging wife."

"I was not nagging! I was merely pointing out—"

"The obvious. And one thing about you, Jenny, is that whatever else you may be, you aren't obvious."

"Thank you." She decided to accept his words as a compliment despite her suspicion that they'd been nothing of the kind.

"You didn't tell me how you liked my car."

Jenny shrugged. "To me a car is four wheels and an engine that gets you from point A to point B. This thing may get you there, but that's all it'll do. There's no room in it to haul anything." Or anyone. She paused as she suddenly realized that the Corvette had only two seats. Nick had purposely bought a car that excluded Jed.

Get a grip on your imagination, Jenny Ryton, she thought, pulling herself up short. All Nick had done was buy something he'd always wanted. She very much doubted whether anything else, especially one small boy he didn't particularly like, had even been considered. And there was no reason she or Jed should have been considered. Jenny ignored the frisson of hurt that feathered through her mind. Her and Nick's association was purely temporary. The car would outlive their marriage by many years.

Nick pulled into the almost deserted church parking lot, turned off the engine and came around to open her door. "You do have the license, don't you?" he asked as they walked up the shallow church steps.

"I gave it to Reverend Marston when he was in the shop." She stepped through the heavy oak doors Nick held open and then jumped as the triumphant strains of Purcell's *Trumpet Voluntary* poured out of the organ loft, reverberating through the large brick building. The interior lights suddenly flicked on to reveal approximately two hundred people sitting in the pews, smiling happily at them.

What did Jenny think she was doing? Nick wondered angrily. He'd agreed to marry her. He'd even managed to contain his annoyance at the fact that she hadn't had the gumption to simply tell the minister that they wanted a civil ceremony. But this was too much. He gripped her arm and turned her toward him. The shadows in the vestibule hid his expression from the guests, if not from Jenny.

"Why the hell did you do this!"

"I didn't! All I agreed to was to have Reverend Marston marry us here in the church. I didn't know anything about this, Nick. I swear."

"Ten to one, there's the culprit." Nick nodded grimly at the plump figure hurrying down the center aisle.

Jenny turned as Marge reached them. The older woman handed her a huge bouquet of cream roses and then gave her a quick hug.

"Are you surprised?" Marge demanded.

"You might say that," Nick said tightly.

"Men." Marge dismissed his obvious annoyance with a sniff. "They'll always slide out of a big wedding if they can. But when I talked to your mother, she was so upset that your father's doctor advised against flying up for the ceremony that I said I'd organize everything for her. She was determined that you should have a day to remember."

"Oh, I'll remember it," Jenny said with absolute truth. Whether or not she would survive it was another matter. She could feel the tension emanating from Nick's large body, but she didn't see what she could do about it. She could hardly stalk out of the church and refuse to get married simply because a lot of her friends wanted to wish her well. And neither could he. Jenny remembered Nick's new car with a feeling of relief. He had to go through with their marriage in order to get the money to pay for it.

She forced herself to listen to Marge's instructions on walking up the aisle in time to the music. Instructions that Nick ignored as he stalked toward the altar, his relentless hold on her arm forcing her to keep pace. Jenny glanced uneasily at the pews of smiling people and then relaxed as she saw their benign expressions. Quite obviously they were interpreting his speed as eagerness to marry her. A feeling of contrition filled her at the expression of loving satisfaction on the face of one of her elderly great-aunts, causing her to miss a step. Somehow, their marriage seemed so much more serious in a church with all her friends and relatives gathered around her than it had when all that had been involved was a quick trip to the justice of the peace.

Nick's grip on her arm tightened as he steadied her for a second against his body. The muscles of his thigh pressed into hers, and the slightly scratchy material of his pant leg scraped over her nylon-clad calf, sending a wave of tremors through her. She quickly regained her balance and moved away fractionally, but the scent of his cologne pursued her, engulfing her in a tangy cloud of masculinity.

When they reached the altar, Jenny glanced back over the pews and her gaze collided with Jed's steel-gray regard. The inimical expression in the depths of his eyes poured over her like a bucket of icy water.

Don't look like that, Jed. She sent him a pleading glance. She wished she could tell him that all they had to do was hang in there for a year, but she couldn't. Not and maintain the fiction that this was a normal marriage. She set her bouquet down and turned back to the minister, who opened the small leather prayer book he was holding and began the age-old service.

"... All of you to join us in the church basement for the reception." Reverend Marston's final words jerked Jenny out of her feelings of relief that this afternoon's ordeal was almost over. It appeared she'd been premature in her self-congratulations. She stole a quick glance at Nick's incredulous expression, and any hope she'd been harboring that she'd imagined the words died stillborn.

"Oh, Reverend Marston, we aren't ... I mean ... there isn't ..." she stammered, hoping that he'd simply forgotten and used his standard wedding closing. He hadn't.

"Of course there's a reception." He beamed at her. "Marge and the Ladies' Aid Society organized it. You didn't think we wouldn't give you a proper send-off, Jenny? Not after you've been such a help to the church for so many years. As I'm sure you will continue to be, especially now that you have a husband to join you." He peered over the top of his bifocals at Nick, who, Jenny noted with malicious glee, didn't seem able to tell the minister no, either. Nick merely gave a short nod, pregnant with suppressed emotion.

Ignoring Nick's lack of enthusiasm, Reverend Marston said, "Why don't you two take Jed and go downstairs and prepare to welcome your guests while I say the final prayer."

"Certainly." Jenny grasped the opportunity to escape, even if it was only temporary. She held a hand out for Jed as they passed the front pew, pretending not to notice the way he scooted around her to avoid walking beside Nick.

"We'd better stand at the bottom of the stairs and greet each person as they come in," Jenny said, planning as they descended the steps.

"Maybe, if we're quick about it, they won't have time to ask questions that are none of their business," Nick said sourly.

"Optimist." Jenny grinned. "Since when's that ever stopped them? Come on, Jed, you stand between us."

"No!" Jed gritted out. "I won't." With a glare at Nick he stomped off to a corner of the room.

"I'm sorry," she apologized. "He just needs a little time."

"Personally, my vote goes for a smack on the seat of his pants." Nick frowned at the boy. "But for now…" He turned toward the people hurrying down the stairs.

"Jenny, dear." Her great-aunt Agnes kissed her. "I'm so happy for you, dear. It's just a shame your poor mother couldn't be here to see you finally married."

Jenny ignored both Nick's smothered laughter and the implications in the word "finally." "Thank you, Aunt Agnes. We're hoping that Dad's new medication stabilizes his blood pressure so that they'll be able to visit us over Christmas."

"That's good news." Iva Warring, whose tenure as librarian stretched beyond Jenny's memory, spoke up. "I really miss your folks, Jenny. Things don't seem the same since they moved to Florida. Now, Nick, if your mother were to decide to fly home for the holidays instead of staying the whole year in New Zealand with Angie and her family, it would be like old times."

"Almost." Sadness colored Nick's voice as he remembered his father, who would never again join a family celebration.

"As long as he lives in your heart, he'll be present, Nick." Father Bauer, the pastor of St. Mary's, gave him a comforting pat on the shoulder.

"Father," Jenny greeted him with pleasure, "it was good of you to come."

"Wouldn't have missed it. I always thought the pair of you were well matched."

"Hmm." Jenny refused to ask what he'd based his opinion on. He was liable to tell her.

"How do you like the reception, Jenny?" Marge beamed at her.

"You and the Ladies' Aid Society shouldn't have bothered," Jenny stated with absolute conviction.

"Nonsense, you deserve the best, and it wasn't that much trouble. The hardest part was getting everyone to park in the city lot so you wouldn't see the cars and suspect something. Honestly—" Marge grimaced "—the younger ones were the worst. They never walk anywhere. I think it's so romantic that the two of you corresponded all those years. Why, I never suspected a thing." She gave them one last smile and moved on.

"Corresponded?" Nick whispered in Jenny's ear.

"Well, I had to say something and the truth wouldn't do," she whispered back.

"Now, now, none of that," Nick's aunt Maggie bellowed. "You'll have plenty of time for cuddling later. And a good thing, too. This family's dying out. But mind you, no kids for nine months."

"Um, yes, ma'am." Jenny flushed. Whoever had said that the older generation was reserved about sex obviously hadn't belonged to a large family.

"Don't mind Aunt Maggie's bluntness, Jenny," Liz, a cousin of Nick's, said. "She doesn't mean any harm. Besides, if she'd just think, she'd know you couldn't be expecting. Nick hasn't been back long enough."

"How about if I can't be expecting because Nick's morals preclude it?" Jenny said tartly.

"If you believe that, I've got this bridge I'd like to sell you." Liz grinned at her.

"Go eat something, Liz. You're embarrassing Jenny." Nick chuckled.

"Where's Jed, Miss Ryton?" Bryan tugged at her sleeve.

"Mrs. Carlton," his mother corrected, and Jenny shivered at the sound of her new title. Somehow, being called by Nick's name made their marriage seem so much more real.

"Mrs. Carlton, then. Where's Jed?" Bryan demanded impatiently.

"Try the refreshment table," Jenny suggested.

"He said he wouldn't stand next to him." Bryan glanced disdainfully at Nick. "He said he didn't like him."

"He said entirely too much," Nick replied. "Don't you make the same mistake."

"No, sir." Bryan gulped and, with an apprehensive look at Nick, backed out of line.

"Don't mind him." Sarah Pearson, Bryan's mother, shrugged. "Despite what they say, kids are a lot more conservative than adults. They hate change."

"You can say that again," Barbara Witson, Sarah's sister-in-law, groaned. "My son hated his new stepfather when I remarried."

"How long did it take for him to accept him?" Jenny asked curiously.

"I don't know, it's only been three years."

"Thanks, I needed that." Jenny sighed.

"Don't mind me. I'm just a little soured on marriage at the moment. Although I can see why you aren't." She gave Nick a sidelong, flirtatious glance that Jenny unexpectedly found irritating.

"Come on, sister-in-law," Sarah said. "It's bad manners to ogle the bridegroom."

"I'd like to do a whole lot more than just ogle him." Barbara's answer was clearly audible as they moved away, but Jenny pretended not to hear as she turned to greet the next guest. She didn't care what Nick got up to, she told herself, trying hard to believe it.

"It was kind of you to come, Mayor Eardly." Jenny managed not to wince as he crushed her hand in his.

"Not at all, Jenny, not at all. Glad you're back, m'boy," he said to Nick. "Too many of our young people leave."

"For many it's an economic necessity," Nick replied.

"True," the mayor conceded. "Not everyone's got a nice farm like yours. What crops are you putting in?"

"I haven't decided."

"You'll be needing equipment, whatever it is. You sold it all when your dad died, didn't you?"

"Not exactly. I let my cousin Sam have it."

"Old Jessic's retiring, and he's auctioning off his machinery next week. Why don't you go?"

"I'll see," Nick said, and Mayor Eardly, with a speculative look at him, moved on. A speculation that was shared by Jenny. Why hadn't Nick jumped at the chance to pick up some farm machinery cheaply? she wondered.

She suddenly caught sight of Jed. He was talking to Bryan, and it didn't take a mind reader to guess what he was saying. The faintly shocked, faintly amused faces of the adults around him were evidence enough.

Jenny breathed a sigh of relief as she saw Marge purposefully make her way toward Jed.

"That young man's nose is out of joint," Mrs. Luftus, an old friend of Nick's mother, observed.

"He's never behaved like this before," Jenny said weakly.

"There was no reason. He's always had his own way before," Nick murmured in a voice that boded ill for Jed. Jenny forced back a sharp retort. Jed was giving the guests enough to talk about. She had no intention of adding to it. Determinedly she turned back to welcoming her guests. The sooner the reception was over, the sooner she could get out of there and try to put her life back into some semblance of normalcy.

4

"THAT'S IT." Nick watched the last guest move toward the refreshment table. "Let's get out of here."

"We really ought to mingle a bit." Jenny's sense of social obligation warred with her natural inclination to escape an impossible situation.

"And field a few more pointed questions about the suddenness of our marriage?"

Or about how lucky she was to be marrying Nick Carlton, she thought, unsure of which was worse. She felt like such a hypocrite accepting all her friends' good wishes.

"Besides," Nick continued, "they'll certainly understand our wanting to get away. They were all young once. In fact, I'm not so sure some of them have grown up yet." He glanced in resignation at his aunt Maggie.

"Shh. This is no time to be dredging up the truth. They'..." She paused as she watched Jed's thin face darken with anger at something the boy standing next to him was saying.

"Uh-oh." She hurried over to him. All this wedding needed to cap it off was for Jed to punch one of the guests.

"Enjoying yourself, Jed?" Her voice held a faint warning.

"Tim and I were just going outside." Jed glared at the other boy.

"Can't." Tim shrugged. "These are my good clothes, and my mom, she'd kill me if I ripped them."

"You'd better—"

"Not now, Jed." Jenny cut him off.

"All right, but you're still a liar, Tim Grant!"

"Am not," Tim muttered with a sidelong glance at Jenny. "You ask Steve. He'll tell you the same thing." With a triumphant look at Jed Tim escaped.

"I should have beat him up!" Jed's voice cracked from the strength of his feelings.

"All that would prove is who's stronger. Not who's right."

"He isn't right, is he?" Jed looked at her with misery-filled eyes.

"That rather depends on what he said."

"He said . . . that now that you had *him*—" Jed shot a resentful glance across the room at Nick, who'd been waylaid by the organist "—you wouldn't want me anymore."

"Wouldn't want . . ." Jenny closed her eyes in despair. How could what had seemed like such a straightforward solution to her problem of getting custody of Jed have developed so many complications?

"Nick is my husband and you are my son," she finally said. "You both have your own place in my heart. A place that can't be usurped."

"But which do you love the best?" Jed demanded.

"You can't measure a person's feelings, Jed. I love my parents, too, but that doesn't mean that I love you any less."

"That's different, they—" He broke off as Nick joined them.

"Jed, Mrs. Norris is going to bring you home when she's ready to leave."

"I'm going with Jenny." Jed moved closer to her.

"My car only seats two," Nick said.

"I can squeeze in beside Jenny."

"No seat belt, no ride," Nick stated flatly.

"I—" Jed began hotly.

"However, I could take Jenny home and then come back for you," Nick offered.

"Ride home alone with you!" Jed's voice rose, and Jenny was embarrassingly aware of sympathetic looks being directed at her.

"Oh, I'm safe enough. Usually." Nick's voice hardened slightly, and even Jed caught the warning.

"Don't bother. I'll go with Mrs. Norris." Jed stomped away.

"Jed!" Jenny started after him, but Nick grabbed her arm and started toward the stairs.

"You're about to make a tactical error," he told her. "Never give in to emotional blackmail."

"But he's upset."

"Who isn't?" Nick said ruefully, escorting her out of the church's front door. "If I had had any idea what your friend was up to . . ."

"I know. But Marge meant well."

"How does that old saying go? About the road to hell being paved with good intentions?"

"I wouldn't know. I've never been there." Jenny slipped into the low-slung sports car.

"How about heaven?" Nick gave her a crooked grin that accelerated her heartbeat. Instinctively Jenny knew what he was referring to. The gleam in her husband's eyes was as explicit as any picture.

Her husband. She examined the words, exploring the weight and taste of them. Her husband. The phrase seemed to echo through her mind. Her attention was caught by the movement of Nick's long, tanned fingers as they gripped the black steering wheel. He had big hands. Strong hands.

The feel of those hands holding her captive against him welled out of her subconscious, and she hastily refocused, her gaze landing on his thigh and tracing the powerful

muscles straining against the fine gray fabric of his pants.
Compulsively her attention moved upward, lingering on
the flat stomach visible beneath his unbuttoned suit jacket.
He was such a large man. Was he large all over? The fugitive thought unexpectedly popped into her mind.

"Jenny, wake up."

"What?" She blinked, looking around in surprise. They
were parked in front of her quilt shop.

"Poor Jenny." Nick ran his fingertips along her jawline
and then cupped her chin in his hand.

She could feel the callused surface of his palm scraping
abrasively over her soft skin. Whatever he'd been doing in
the Middle East, he'd used his hands to do it, she realized,
trying to concentrate on that thought instead of the strange,
shivery sensation radiating from his touch. His thumb
rubbed over her soft lower lip, tugging it downward.

Jenny risked a peek into his lean face and then wished she
hadn't when her gaze became entrapped in the silvery lights
dancing in the depths of his bright blue eyes. She watched,
filled with a confusing mixture of anticipation and dread as
they came closer, until she felt as if she were drowning in an
azure sea. His lips stopped a fraction of an inch from hers,
and a tremor of longing skipped through her.

The tip of his tongue darted out to lightly flick across the
closed line of her lips, and they instinctively parted, an action Nick was quick to take advantage of. His mouth closed
over hers, and he used his body to pin her against her seat.

She touched his face, intending to push him away, but the
feel of his skin took her by surprise and she found her fingers lingering, slowly sliding across the raspy silk of his
freshly shaved cheek. With a will of their own her fingers
threaded their way through the crisp strands of his hair and
tugged him closer. His tongue surged between her lips, ag-

gressively stroking over hers. A moan of mindless pleasure bubbled out of her throat.

"Ah, Jenny, you smell so good." The clean warmth of his breath wafted across the skin of her face, causing it to tighten in reaction.

"So do you," she muttered, her eyes reluctantly opening to find him watching her with a curious intensity. Embarrassed, she focused on his elegantly knotted tie and made a mental retreat, her only option since his embrace cut off a physical one.

"But despite our mutual attraction, I think we'd best save it for later." He slowly released her.

"I don't . . ." She ground to a halt under the knowing gleam in his eyes. He was much too experienced not to have realized exactly what her response to him had been.

"Very wise, Jenny." He lightly flicked the tip of her nose with a gentle fingertip. "Whatever else we may or may not have in this marriage of ours, let's at least have total honesty."

"Total honesty is a trap for fools and idealists."

"Well, I'm definitely not an idealist, and no one's ever called me a fool. So how about if we try for half and half?"

"Half and half?" She frowned uncomprehendingly at him.

"You tell me the truth, and I'll tell you what you want to hear," he elaborated.

"Listen, you patronizing, overbearing—"

"Maybe we should simply skip the truth all around if that's your opinion of me." He chuckled.

"There's no need." She looked down her nose at him. "I'll simply remember to make allowances for you because you are what you are."

"I know I'm going to be sorry I asked, but what am I?"

"A man at the mercy of his rather primitive urges."

"Well, if you're willing to make allowances for that . . ." He grabbed her and pulled her across the gearshift into his lap.

"Nick!" Jenny squeaked a second before his mouth covered hers, swallowing the sound of her outrage. A wave of excitement crashed through her as his warm hand slipped under her skirt to curve around her thigh.

Her eyes flew open at the intimacy of his touch, and she found herself staring into his mischief-filled eyes.

"Nicholas Sylvester Carlton!" She ineffectually tried to push aside his hand, which was showing an alarming tendency to creep upward.

"But, Jenny, you agreed to make allowances for my primitive urges." He gave her a look of mock astonishment.

"I'll make you!"

"Now you're talking." He grinned, and Jenny felt a fiery blush scorch her face. Blast Nick! He not only made her feel like an adolescent, he was making her act like one, too.

"This has gone far enough," she said tightly.

"All things considered, you're probably right," he said with a rueful glance toward the shop.

Jenny followed his glance and then groaned when she saw the avidly watching face in the shop window.

"Who's the voyeur?" Nick made no move to stop her when she scooted off his lap.

"Elsie Wyvern. She married Ed Collings, Bill Staten and Curt Vinton."

"Obviously a lady worth knowing." Nick chuckled.

"Why not? Every other man in town has!" she bit out and was immediately ashamed of the catty remark. Taking a deep breath, she said, "Forget I said that."

"You mean it isn't true?"

"Sure it's true. I just shouldn't have said it. Although, knowing Elsie, you'll be able to judge for yourself. She'll probably be out in a second to give you the once-over."

"Not me. I'm a married man," he said self-righteously. "Hurry up and get out of the car so I can escape."

Jenny did, torn between a desire not to expose him to what seemed to be Elsie's fatal fascination with the male sex and an inexplicable longing to keep him close.

"I'm going out to the farm to get my clothes." He put the car in reverse. "Don't fix dinner. I'll take you out."

"But we can't leave Jed alone," she protested.

He shrugged. "So line up a baby-sitter."

"We could all go out to dinner," she suggested.

"We were just married, Jenny," he said impatiently. "Jed's hardly going to be surprised if we want to eat alone. I'll be back shortly." He pulled away.

"Damn!" Jenny swore at the dilemma she found herself in. If she and Nick went out, then Jed would feel even more displaced and she couldn't allow that to happen. No matter how much she wanted to go. And she did want to go, she admitted honestly. Much as she loved Jed, there was something about Nick that drew her.

It's called sex, she thought, making a valiant attempt to put her unprecedented reaction to Nick into some kind of perspective.

She pushed open the shop door and walked in. Letty was standing beside Elsie at the window.

"Oh, Jenny, he's gorgeous." Letty sighed rapturously. "Exactly like Sir Laurence Olivier in the movie we saw in English class last week. All dark and brooding." She shivered dramatically.

"Sorry to disillusion you, Letty, but Nick Carlton doesn't brood; he yells. Loudly."

"Nick Carlton?" Elsie queried. "I think he went to school with my husband."

"Which one?" Jenny asked innocently.

"What's he doing back in this hick town?" Elsie ignored the question.

"Marrying me. I'm surprised you didn't know. Everybody else seemed to." Jenny grimaced, remembering the crowd at the church.

"I just got back from Elmira today. I've been staying with a friend. Well, I'll be seeing you, Jenny." Elsie gave her a feline smile and sauntered out.

Jenny watched her go, filled with a vague sense of apprehension.

"Do you still want me to stay until closing, Jenny?" Letty asked.

"If you would, please. I have some things to do upstairs. Call if you need anything." Jenny scurried up the back stairs, anxious to have a few minutes to herself.

Once she was dressed in her familiar jeans and sweater, she felt more like her normal self. She debated going back down to the shop, but the thought of having to face Letty's romantic sighs held no appeal. Besides, she realized as she caught sight of the time, it was hardly worth it. They closed in half an hour.

The sound of a car door slamming caught her attention and she peered out the living room window into the parking lot below. Nick was taking his luggage out of his Corvette.

The sight of the car reminded her that she hadn't given him his check, and after that afternoon he'd certainly earned it. She dug it out of her purse as Nick shouldered open the front door. He stepped inside and glanced around.

"Where's our bedroom?" he asked.

"Our bedroom?" Jenny's fingers tightened around the check as his words sent a curl of excitement through her. Careful not to let her feelings show on her face, she nodded toward the hallway. "It's the door on the right."

Slowly she followed him into the room. Not large to begin with, it seemed to shrink under the dynamic impact of Nick's vibrant personality.

"The kid back yet?" he asked.

"No, *Jed* is not back yet!" she snapped, annoyed at the impersonal way Nick always referred to him.

"Having second thoughts already, wife?" His lips lifted in a smile that had no foundation in humor. Their grim twist sent an apprehensive shiver down her spine as it suddenly occurred to her that Nick Carlton would be a very formidable enemy. Moreover, from the bite in his voice it was clear that today's events had been as much of a strain for him as they had been for her.

"No, Nick, I'm not having second thoughts," she said soothingly. "As a matter of fact, I've got your check right here." She held it out to him.

He dropped his garment bag on the bed, his suitcase on the floor and took the check, his mind automatically cataloging her trembling as his fingers brushed hers.

Desire or fear? Nick studied her, his attention lingering on the abnormal brightness of her huge brown eyes. She looked like someone who was at the end of her tether. As if she were just beginning to realize the full ramifications of what their marriage entailed. He stifled a sigh. Although she'd listened when he'd tried to tell her what it would be like to be married to him, she hadn't really heard.

His gaze was drawn to the proud thrust of her small breasts under the soft green sweater she was wearing. They'd fit exactly into the palm of his hand. He clenched his fingers as he felt his body stir in response to his thoughts and he hastily clamped down on them. Jenny needed time to get used to him before he made any emotional demands on her. And he had lots of time. His face hardened. He couldn't even begin to make definite plans for the future until he was sure Don was going to be freed. Not when it was his fault that Don had been kidnapped in the first place.

"Is something wrong with the check?" Jenny asked anxiously. It was what they'd agreed to. So why was he looking so grim?

"No, it's fine." He shoved the check in his pocket and turned toward the closet.

An unexpected feeling of disappointment feathered through her. *What'd you expect? For him to refuse the money and declare he'd married you for old times' sake?* she mocked her reaction. No, it was much better that they stick to their original agreement. A flush tinted her cheeks as her gaze dropped to the bed and she remembered another part of their agreement.

"Jenny?" Jed's querulous voice provided a welcome escape from the claustrophobic atmosphere of the small bedroom.

She gave Nick a bright social smile and said, "I'll leave you to unpack while I see what he wants."

"Is he here?" Jed demanded and Jenny grimaced. Honestly, what a pair. To Nick Jed was "the kid," and to Jed Nick was "he."

"There are times, my lad, when I wish I'd become a nun." She picked up the suit jacket Jed had flung on the sofa.

"You can't be a nun. You're a Methodist. Although there was something in the paper yesterday about an Episcopalian minister in Erie, Pennsylvania, who was married and then became a Catholic priest. I wonder what his new congregation calls his wife? Mother?"

"Try courageous," Jenny said dryly. "What took you so long?"

"Mrs. Norris took me to the nursing home so I could give Gramma a piece of the wedding cake. She cried."

"Is her hip bothering her?"

"Not the hurting kind of crying. The soppy kind because Mrs. Norris told her all about the wedding."

"Ladies like to cry at weddings." Jenny's lips twitched at Jed's disgusted expression.

"Jenny?" He fiddled with the end of his tie. "When I was coming back from getting Gramma a plate for her cake, I heard her tell Mrs. Norris that it would be nice for you to have a husband to help with the worry of raising me. Jenny, am I a burden to you?" he finished in a rush.

"Oh, Jed." Jenny looked down into his thin face. "Don't you know that I love you? I've certainly told you often enough."

"But am I a burden?" he insisted.

Jenny studied his worried eyes and decided on complete honesty rather than a facile lie.

"In one sense, loving someone is always a burden. Especially a child because you become responsible for him. But, Jed, if I hadn't wanted you, I wouldn't have asked Social Services for custody. I didn't have to take you, you know."

"You mean like Melba?"

"Melba?" Jenny repeated blankly.

"Uh-huh. Ryan, who sits next to me in school, his mom had another baby girl. The third." His expression clearly showed what he thought of that particular piece of idiocy. "And Ryan said that his mom yelled and yelled at his dad and said it was all his fault and she didn't want another baby. But they had to keep it, anyway."

"Um, Jed, Ryan shouldn't have told you that. And you most definitely shouldn't be repeating it."

"Why not, if it's the truth? But what I don't understand is why his mom got pregnant if she didn't want another baby? I mean, that book we read explained what to do if you want babies, so if you don't want any, why would you do it?"

Jenny closed her eyes in dismay. Right now she simply wasn't up to explaining to a precocious nine-year-old that sex encompassed a whole lot more than procreation.

"Well, you see, Jed . . ." She stared down into his puzzled gray eyes. Eyes that suddenly narrowed with anger as he caught sight of Nick standing in Jenny's bedroom door.

Deliberately Jed moved closer to her and demanded, "What's he doing in your room?"

"Unpacking." She tried to sound casual.

"But that's your room," Jed insisted.

"Husbands and wives generally sleep in the same room," Nick said.

"Be grateful." Jenny tried for a light touch. "The only other bedroom is yours."

"I don't want to share with him!"

"Then it all worked out for the best," Jenny said, but quite obviously Jed didn't share her sentiments. His eyes swung from Jenny back to Nick.

"Do you want any babies?" He shot the question at Nick.

"Absolutely not!" Nick's face hardened as he remembered Adelaide's coming baby. One child mixed up in this mess was more than enough.

"I guess it's all right, then." Jed headed for his room.

Jenny stared down at the deep beige carpeting as she struggled with a feeling of embarrassment that was almost tangible. And underlying that was an irrational sense of hurt. Of course they didn't want any babies out of this mock marriage, but did Nick have to sound so emphatic about it? As if she were the last person he'd ever consider as the mother of his children.

"What are you looking for down there?" Nick walked over to her.

"My composure," she said wryly.

"It's your own fault. If you hadn't told him the facts of life . . ."

"He wouldn't know?" she scoffed. "That's ridiculous."

"Oh, I don't know. Whatever happened to the stork?"

"The rampant teenage pregnancy rate! You wouldn't believe the misconceptions that kids grow up with when their parents opt out of their responsibilities."

"I hardly think—"

"You haven't had to! You don't have kids. But let me tell you, no child of mine is going to grow up thinking that it's safe the first time or that you can't get pregnant if you do it standing up."

"You mean you can?" Nick's eyes glowed with devilment.

"Don't tease me. I happen to feel very strongly about this."

"You seem to feel very strongly about lots of things and all of them are tied up with that kid." He gestured toward Jed's closed bedroom door. "You need to diversify your emotional expenditures a little." He gave a slow, sensual smile.

Jenny blinked under the force of it and hastily backtracked. "I'm sure you're not interested in—"

"All men are interested in—"

"I meant . . ." She paused in relief as the phone interrupted a conversation that was showing definite signs of getting out of hand.

Picking up the receiver, she said, "Hello?"

There was a brief second of silence, and then a woman's voice hesitantly asked, "Is Nick Carlton there?"

Jenny frowned, trying to place the voice, but she couldn't. The muffled tones, as if the woman had a heavy cold, made it difficult to even make an accurate guess as to her age.

"It's for you." Jenny handed the phone to Nick. "She didn't give a name."

"Thanks, Jenny. Hello? Yes, Adelaide. No, of course, you aren't bothering me."

There was no "of course" about it, Jenny thought in annoyance as she went into the kitchen. What kind of woman called a man on his wedding day?

She opened the refrigerator door and stared blindly inside, her mind still on the phone call. Adelaide wasn't that common a name. She didn't know anyone in town with it. But then it didn't have to be a local call. If the woman had dialed direct, it could be from anywhere, including the Middle East. Was this Adelaide somehow connected with Nick's old job?

Jenny turned and surreptitiously studied Nick, listening to the sound of his voice rising and falling in soothing murmurs. Whoever this Adelaide was, Nick obviously liked her. That much was evident from his tone.

Hurriedly she turned back to the refrigerator as he hung up.

"What are you looking for in there? Frostbite?" Nick asked.

"Something to fix for dinner. I don't think I know anyone named Adelaide?" She tried to probe.

"Don't you? Well, the next time we're in New York, I'll introduce you to the only Adelaide I know. You don't have to fix dinner." He changed the subject before she could ask any more questions. "I told you I was taking you out."

"And I told you that I refuse to leave Jed alone on your first night here." She forgot the unknown Adelaide in her concern for Jed.

Nick gently moved her aside and pushed the refrigerator door closed. He was appalled by the tension he could feel in her slender body. He'd been right. She did need time to learn to relax around him. And Adelaide's phone call certainly hadn't helped. Jenny was clearly curious about her, but there was no point in his explaining the situation to her now. Not when it appeared that Murad was going to be able to successfully negotiate Don's release. He wanted to lessen Jenny's worries, not add to them. And he could start by including Jed in his dinner plans, he decided.

"We'll take the kid with us. He can even pick out the restaurant," Nick offered. "I can survive hamburgers for one night."

"Your car doesn't seat three." Jenny warily reminded him. Why had he changed his mind? Earlier he'd been emphatic in his refusal to take Jed with them. Now he was suddenly willing to put up with him. Was it somehow connected with the phone call from Adelaide?

"So we use your Caravan."

"All right." Jenny agreed, knowing that it was in everyone's best interests if she met him halfway.

5

"DRAT!" JENNY WATCHED in exasperation as the egg yolk oozed across the frying pan. Scraping it out of the skillet, she dropped it into the garbage.

"What's the matter?" Jed asked.

"I broke the yolk of Nick's egg," she murmured, carefully slipping another into the sizzling butter.

"But you always tell me to eat it, anyway." His face set in lines of outrage. "You said it was the luck of the draw and we shouldn't waste good food."

"Well, yes, but . . ." Jenny paused, wondering why kids always remembered what you'd told them at the most inconvenient moment possible. She could hardly tell Jed the truth. That she was trying very hard to convince Nick that joining their family, even on a temporary basis, had been a good idea. A fact Nick must be doubting, considering Jed's attitude of unrelieved belligerence.

"He . . ." Jed fell silent as Nick walked into the kitchen.

"What's for breakfast?" Nick leaned over her shoulder and peered down into the frying pan.

A fine tension tightened her muscles as the tang of the soap he'd just used engulfed her. It was a reaction she was at a loss to explain. The scent of the same soap on Jed induced nothing more than a feeling of satisfaction that he'd remembered to wash.

She glanced sideways at Nick, taking in the well-worn jeans that hugged the powerful muscles of his thighs. Her attention skittered upward past his flat stomach to his broad chest, which was lightly covered by a tattered gray sweat-shirt with the blurred logo Litton High Panthers printed on it.

"That sweatshirt must be twenty years old." She looked askance at it. "And it looks every day of it. I'll buy you another the next time I'm downtown."

"I didn't buy this one." For a second Nick sounded like Jed in one of his more precise moods. "I earned it by making the football team."

"You played football?" Jed demanded.

"For four years." Nick poured himself a glass of orange juice and sat down at the small kitchen table.

"Did you ever get into a game?" Jed sneered.

"He never got out of a game." Jenny set a stack of his favorite blueberry pancakes in front of the boy. "Nick was the best fullback Litton High ever had."

"Why haven't I heard of him, then?" Jed asked suspiciously.

"I imagine there are one or two things that you haven't discovered yet." Jenny breathed a sigh of relief as she managed to get Nick's egg onto his plate without breaking it. She added bacon and two pecan muffins still hot from the oven and handed it to him.

"Thanks, Jenny. It looks delicious." Nick picked up his fork.

"You forgot to say grace. Again," Jed said smugly.

"I do seem to have a lot of trouble remembering what I have to be thankful for, don't I?" Nick's voice was even, but Jenny caught the undercurrents of anger. Wearily she rubbed her forehead. She felt as if she were camped in the middle of a battlefield, what with Jed taking potshots at Nick every chance he got. The fact that Nick was showing such phenomenal patience with Jed only made her more nervous. No one could be that forebearing forever. It simply wasn't possible. Sooner or later Nick was going to explode, and when he did . . . Her stomach twisted nervously. If she managed to come out of this experience without ulcers, it would be a miracle, she thought with a flash of her normal humor.

"What about your own breakfast, Jenny?" Nick frowned at the cup of coffee she was holding.

"I'm not hungry," she said truthfully.

"Breakfast is the most important meal of the day," Nick stated emphatically. "You have to have something."

"Jenny says she's not hungry," Jed rushed to defend her.

"And you're not thinking." Nick gave him a look that effectively silenced him.

"I'll eat later." *Once I've recovered from breakfast with the pair of you*, she thought ruefully. "That's one of the nice things about living above your work. You can slip upstairs whenever you want," she said with a forced brightness that sat oddly in the tense atmosphere.

But would she? Nick wondered with a thoughtful look at her strained features. He could almost see the tension in her slim fingers as she gripped her coffee cup. Poor Jenny. She was finding this marriage even more of a strain than he was. He shifted uncomfortably as his body instinctively reacted to his perusal of her body. This past week had been almost impossible, sleeping beside her and yet not reaching out to pull her to him. Not stripping off the long flannel nightgown that hid her curves. A nightgown he was almost certain she'd chosen in the hope of disguising her attractions. Not that she'd succeeded. Jenny would look good in a gunnysack.

Maybe he was wrong in waiting to put their marriage on a more natural footing. Maybe he was merely adding to her anxiety. He glanced over at her, his eyes lingering on her soft pink lips. He watched as their corners lifted fractionally.

What was she thinking? he wondered. It was impossible to tell. The girl he remembered whose every thought had been clearly written on her face had matured into a highly complex woman with unexpected depths to her personality. Depths that he was looking forward to plumbing with a great deal of anticipation.

JENNY GLANCED UP from the material she was cutting for Mrs. Blackmore as the shop door opened and Elsie Wyvern sauntered in. Jenny stifled a sigh. She simply wasn't in the mood to parry off-color remarks that morning.

"So how's the happy bride these days?" Elsie gave Jenny a sly grin. "Getting enough sleep?"

"Certainly. I'm very fortunate. Nick doesn't snore."

"Speaking of Nick—" Elsie looked around the crowded shop "—I haven't seen him lately."

"He doesn't work in the shop," Jenny said unhelpfully. It was bad enough that Elsie was interested in him. Surely the woman didn't expect his own wife to help her in her pursuit.

"Then where—"

"Jenny." To Jenny's relief Mrs. Blackmore interrupted. "Make that four yards of the yellow instead of three. I think I'll make a couple of crib pillows, too."

"Who's having a baby?" Marge's glance automatically swung to Jenny, who ignored her. What was the matter with everyone this week? They all seemed to have exactly one thing on their minds. Sex. At least everyone except Nick, she thought uneasily. Despite his insistence that theirs was to be marriage in every sense of the word, he'd made no effort to even begin to deepen the emotional currents that swirled between them.

But why? she wondered for at least the hundredth time. Why had he changed his mind? As far as she could tell, his

uninterest dated from the phone call he'd received from
Adelaide on their wedding day. Was he having an affair with
the woman? But that didn't really make any sense. Nick had
offered to introduce Adelaide to her the next time they were
in the city. Moreover, his tone when he'd been talking to
Adelaide hadn't sounded fraught with passion. He'd
sounded . . . supportive, she finally decided. But supportive of what? Mentally she shook her head, dismissing the
whole thing.

"My son, Marcus." Mrs. Blackmore's ample bosom
seemed to swell with pride.

"I always knew that Marcus was clever, but imagine him
figuring out how to have a baby all by himself." Jenny
laughed.

"Don't tease your elders, Jenny." Mrs. Blackmore gently
reproved her. "I'm so excited, I don't know whether I'm
coming or going. After all these years I'm finally going to
be a grandmother."

"When's the baby due?" Marge asked.

"Not till the middle of March, so I have lots of time to
make a crib quilt." Mrs. Blackmore smiled in happy anticipation. "I just hope this time I get a real baby."

"A real baby?" Jenny stared at her. "Let me guess. You've
been watching old science fiction films where they substitute aliens for humans?"

"Sometimes it seemed like that." Mrs. Blackmore grimaced. "I don't think Marcus was ever really a child."

"It couldn't have been that bad." Marge looked up from
the notions she was sorting.

"Well, the first eighteen months were great, but then he
started to talk," Mrs. Blackmore said darkly. "I'll never forget the first time I realized that he wasn't quite like other
people's babies. We were standing in the checkout line at the
grocery store. He was about two, and I was trying to amuse

him while we waited our turn. I pointed out the shape of a triangle, said triangle, and he repeated it. Then I identified a square and he said square, and then I showed him a circle and he said elliptical spheroid."

"Was he right?" Marge asked.

"How would I know?" Mrs. Blackmore shrugged. "The point is that I haven't understood him since. Other kids wrote their Christmas list from Sears' *Wish Book*. Marcus used Edmond's Scientific Catalog."

"I know just what you mean." Jenny sighed.

"Maybe the baby will take after Marcus's wife," Marge offered. "What's she like?"

"She's got lovely eyes and she's kind."

"Kind!" Elsie scoffed. "Men don't want kind; they want sexy."

"If she's expecting, Marcus must find her sexy." Jenny frowned at Elsie. "Personally, I think she sounds perfect for him."

"Oh, she is," Mrs. Blackmore agreed. "I just wish she weren't quite so clever. She's a Greek scholar, you know. If it's really true that kids take after their parents . . ."

"That's $27.92, Mrs. Blackmore." Jenny handed her the sack. "And don't worry. Marcus wasn't like you, so chances are the baby won't be like Marcus, either."

"But what about his mother knowing Greek?" Mrs. Blackmore wailed.

"That's no big deal," Jenny comforted her. "Millions of Greeks speak Greek, even tiny little children. It doesn't mean a thing."

"That's true." Mrs. Blackmore brightened. "You're a sweet girl, Jenny." She accepted her change. "You deserve a good husband, and Nick Carlton will be one of the best. I should know. He and Marcus were inseparable when they were growing up."

Jenny watched Elsie and Mrs. Blackmore leave, suddenly realizing just how awkward it was going to be when she and Nick filed for divorce. The phone rang, and grateful for the distraction, she answered it.

"Calico Corners Quilt Shop. Jenny speaking."

"Hi, Jenny. Mayor Eardly here. I've been ringing your flat, but no one answers. Is Nick around?"

"No. I'm not sure where he is," she admitted. Every morning since the wedding he'd left the flat shortly before eight and hadn't returned until dinnertime. She'd assumed that he was spending his time out at the farm, but she hadn't wanted to ask. Not after his crack about nagging wives.

"I'm calling about the Jessic auction. I mentioned it to him at your wedding reception, but I doubt he remembered." The mayor chuckled. "A man isn't thinking about farm machinery on his wedding day. But he shouldn't miss this auction. Not with him trying to get his farm operational again. If you see him, remind him that it's at Jessic's farm at four."

"I will, and thanks for taking the trouble to call, Mayor Eardly."

"No trouble. Nick's father was a good friend of mine. The least I can do is try to give his son a hand. And you tell Nick that if he's strapped for cash, not to worry. The bank'll be glad to loan him money for machinery, and this is a great time to borrow. Interest rates are the lowest they've been in years."

"I'll tell him. Bye." Jenny hung up.

"What'd the mayor want?" Marge asked.

"To remind Nick about the Jessic auction. I wonder if he wanted to go?"

"Why don't you run out to the farm and find out?" Marge suggested. "I can handle things here for a while."

"But Jed'll be home from school shortly."

"I'll keep an eye on Jed till you get back."

"But he's used to me being here." Jenny chewed her lip uncertainly.

"You listen to me, Jenny Carlton. Jed is your son. You only have him a short time, and then he's gone to live his own life. But Nick is your husband. He'll be around permanently. He has to come first."

Jenny shrugged. What Marge said would be true if their marriage were a normal one, but it wasn't. A fact that she could hardly advertise.

"Because if you don't work at your marriage, you're going to wind up like Elsie with a string of ex-husbands."

Jenny laughed. "There aren't a string of unmarried males in Litton, and I haven't the time to go to Elmira to find them."

"Pretty as you are, they'll find you," Marge said loyally. "But you mind what I say."

"Yes, ma'am." Jenny bobbed a mock curtsy. "Like the loyal little wife I am, I'll run out to the farm to give Nick the message. Tell Jed there're brownies cooling on the counter that he can snack on. I shouldn't be too long."

"Take your time," Marge called after her. "We won't have much business this afternoon."

"Probably not," Jenny agreed as she headed toward her car. It was such a lovely September day most people would prefer to be doing something outside rather than shopping. She sniffed the pungent aroma of burning leaves, feeling incredibly lighthearted. Rather like a schoolgirl playing hooky. Now if only Nick hadn't decided to play hooky, too, because if he had, she didn't have the slightest idea where to look for him. The thought gave her pause. She really knew very little about the man she'd married. Other than that he'd been very busy this past week, she noted as she reached the farm. The deeply rutted driveway was a thing of the past. Now fresh blacktop covered it.

Jenny drove around to the back of the house and parked beside Nick's gleaming red Corvette. The newly paved driveway wasn't the only change. Gone were the waist-high weeds. They had been mowed to an inch-high stubble.

A staccato burst of hammering caught her attention, and she turned toward the noise. Shading her eyes with her hand, she squinted in the strong sunlight. There was a carpenter replacing shingles on the barn roof. He could probably tell her where Nick was. She hurried toward him, only to come to a precipitate halt when she got close enough to see that the man precariously perched on the roof was Nick. Was he out of his mind? The barn ridgepole was easily four stories high. If he fell... A chill coursed over her. There had been no one here to even call an ambulance. Of all the irresponsible, idiotic... Anger began to burn away her paralyzing sense of fear.

"Nicholas Sylvester Carlton, you come down from there," she yelled up at him.

Nick peered down at her and spit the nails out of his mouth. "Why?"

"Because you're going to break your fool neck. You haven't the experience to be climbing around a barn roof, and even if you did, there should be someone else around in case of an accident."

"I hardly think—"

"That much is glaringly obvious," she bit out. "You could be killed!"

"You have a very morbid turn of mind."

"I have a very practical turn of mind. Are you coming down?"

"But, Jenny—" he smiled at her, his white teeth gleaming against the deep tan of his lean cheeks "—I'm no longer alone. If I do fall, you can call an ambulance."

"On what?" she snapped. "If there were a phone out here, I wouldn't be here."

"You have aspirations to be a telephone?" he asked mockingly.

"I have aspirations to be taken seriously."

"Perhaps I would, if you'd stop overreacting."

"I'm not—" She paused and took a deep breath as she realized she was yelling. Nick was right. She was overreacting. The question was why? Why should it bother her that he was taking unnecessary risks? Because if he did manage to kill himself, it would complicate Jed's custody case. She refused to look beyond the obvious answer.

"Nick, I drove out here to talk to you. So would you please come down and let me do it?" Despite her efforts, her voice rose slightly.

"Since you ask so nicely." He shoved his hammer into his carpenter's apron and cautiously moved toward the ladder.

Jenny held her breath as Nick slowly made his way down. Her eyes narrowed in concentration as she watched the smooth rippling of muscles under the deeply tanned skin of his back. Droplets of sweat clung to his shoulders, and she could see a damp line extending from his wide leather belt down into his jeans. From her angle beneath him on the ground the swell of his manhood was clearly visible through the well-worn denim. A tight curl of excitement slithered through her mind, and she closed her eyes to dispel the unexpected longing that assailed her.

When she opened them again, Nick was on the ladder that had been propped against the side of the barn. He was about six feet from the ground when the ladder suddenly wobbled.

Jenny instinctively reached for him, her hands curving around his flat buttocks as she tried to hold him steady. Taken off guard by her touch, he jerked sideways and, with a muffled curse, tumbled off the ladder onto the rock-hard ground below.

"Nick!" His name escaped her in an agonized shriek. She scrambled around the ladder, falling onto her knees beside his body, which was stretched out on the dusty ground. "Nick, say something!"

"Hell!"

"I meant something constructive." Tentatively she touched him. His sun-warmed skin acted like a magnet, and without conscious volition she flattened her hands on his broad back, flexing her fingers slightly as a current of awareness surged through her.

His stifled groan effectively doused her reaction.

"Nick, does anything hurt?" she demanded.

"The question is not what hurts. The question is what doesn't hurt."

"I told you it was dangerous to climb that thing yourself."

Nick pressed his lips together against a hot retort. There hadn't been the slightest danger until she'd touched him. Until he'd felt her small hands pressing into his hips. Desire had exploded in his mind, and he'd instinctively jerked sideways, hurtling himself off the ladder. But he could hardly tell her that. He grimaced in self-disgust. It made him sound like an unseasoned stripling.

"Nick, why are you grimacing? Tell me!"

Tell you what? That you make me feel sixteen again. That you . . . His train of thought was shattered as he felt her fingers close around the back of his thigh. A heavy thrust of excitement pierced him, and he could feel his manhood hardening in unconscious response.

"What are you doing?" he asked, but Jenny barely heard his words as she meticulously worked her way down his thigh and over the well-developed muscles of his calf.

"Jenny?" He tensed as she started on the other leg.

"I know this must be painful," she sympathized.

"Oh, it's painful all right." He suddenly flipped onto his back.

Taken by surprise, Jenny fell across his chest. She could feel the heavy masculine warmth of him seeping into her skin, and a tremor of excitement chased through her, scattering her fear.

"I believe it's the French who call it the little death."

"I wouldn't know," she said primly. "One doesn't meet many Frenchmen in Litton, and even if one did, that's hardly a topic for polite conversation."

"There's nothing polite about the way I feel." His arms tightened around her as she attempted to scoot off him.

"Well, it's your own fault," Jenny said distractedly, finding it difficult to concentrate on anything but the exquisite feel of his body beneath hers. Whatever the reason he'd been ignoring her since their wedding, it wasn't because he didn't find her physically attractive. The thought was exhilarating.

"Augh!" Nick suddenly released her, and Jenny scrambled to her feet at his agonized yelp.

"You did break something!" She watched him stagger to his feet.

"Hardly. I was simply being stabbed by the stem of a weed I chopped off earlier. What a mess." He glanced down at himself in disgust. Tiny bits of weeds, grass and dirt clung to his damp skin. "Would you mind driving me back to the flat, Jenny?" He picked up his hammer, which he'd dropped during his fall.

"Of course I will. Do you feel dizzy?"

"No, I don't want to get dirt and twigs all over the interior of the Corvette."

Jenny stared at him, searching his eyes for a fugitive twinkle. There was none. He was serious. He didn't want to mess up his precious Corvette, but he was perfectly willing to molt all over her Caravan. The humor of the situation suddenly struck her, and she almost grinned. It would serve him right if she refused, but everything considered, it would be better if she did drive. That way, if there were any lingering results of his tumble, he'd be safe with her.

But to her relief he appeared normal on the ride home, and her tentative suggestion that they stop by the doctor's office was met with a scornful refusal. Knowing that she was probably overreacting, she didn't try to insist.

"Jed," she called as they entered the apartment.

"He's probably out playing," Nick said, kicking off his worn Adidas.

"Out?" Jenny repeated. "Oh, no! The auction." She suddenly remembered why she'd gone out to the farm in the first place. Nick's tumble off the ladder had completely driven it from her mind.

"The kid likes auctions?"

"No. You."

"I don't like auctions." He turned and began hobbling toward the bathroom.

"Nick, will you listen to me? Mayor Eardly called to remind you of the Jessic auction. It starts in—" she glanced at the time "—ten minutes. If you hurry, you won't miss much."

"No." He continued toward the bathroom.

She trailed along behind him.

"If it's money, Mayor Eardly said the bank would be glad to give you a loan."

"With the farm as collateral, I imagine they would." Nick sat down on the bathroom stool and yanked off his socks. Then he stood and began to unbuckle his belt.

Jenny swallowed, fascinated by the movements of his lean fingers. Tearing her gaze away, she tried again. "You'll need machinery if you're going to put in a spring crop."

"Did I say I was going to plant next spring?"

"Well, no, but..." She paused. She could hardly say that the seventy-five thousand she'd given him wouldn't last forever. Especially not with him buying expensive sports cars. Maybe he was planning on doing what he'd done in the Middle East. Whatever that had been. "Are you going to do what you did in the Middle East?"

"No," he said succinctly, leaving her curiosity unsatisfied.

"So you aren't going to the auction?"

"You, Jenny Carlton, are a very perceptive woman." He slowly pulled his belt free from his dusty jeans.

"A vengeful one, too." She forced her eyes upward to his face. "So don't try any of your sarcasm on me."

"What should I try on you?" His lips lifted in a suggestive grin that had her automatically retreating a step, a reaction that annoyed her.

"Would you like a drink?" She ignored his question.

"If that's all you're offering, I accept. Make it brandy, straight." He casually unzipped his jeans.

Jenny beat a hasty retreat. She wasn't a naive teenager who didn't know anything about men, but neither was she sophisticated enough to stand there while Nick stripped.

Jed still wasn't in the flat, so she hurried down the back stairs to check with Marge, who told her that Jed had gone to Bryan's house to play.

Jenny spent a few minutes in the shop in order to give Nick time to shower before she returned. She filled a juice glass with brandy and sauntered into their bedroom with what she hoped was just the right amount of sangfroid.

Nick was zipping himself into a clean pair of jeans.

This is where I came in, she thought with a flash of wry amusement.

"Here . . ." Her voice emerged sounding faintly strained. She cleared her throat and tried again. "Here's your drink."

"Put it on the dresser, would you? Do you have any antiseptic?"

"Sure. Why?"

"A scratch that stung like the devil when I was showering." He lifted his arm.

Jenny winced in sympathy at the long, angry weal that ran down over his rib cage.

"Just a second." She hurried into the bathroom, washed her hands, found the tube of ointment and then went back into the bedroom to find Nick sipping the brandy. "Let me put it on for you." She uncapped the tube and squeezed some of it out on her fingertip.

Nick set the glass down and lifted his arm, wincing slightly as she began to gently rub the ointment in.

"Maybe you should get a tetanus shot?"

"My shots are up to date."

"Oh," she murmured distractedly. She could feel the hard projection of his ribs through the silken texture of his skin. Without conscious thought she began to trace one of them across his rib cage, stopping when her fingers became entangled in the thick coating of dark brown hair that covered his chest. It rasped over her fingertips, heightening her awareness of him.

Suddenly his hand closed over hers, pressing it flat against his chest. She could feel the steady, pounding rhythm of his heart. A rhythm that seemed to echo through her body. Her own heart began to beat erratically as if trying to adjust itself to his rhythm. She trembled, not with fear but with anticipation.

Her eyes focused on the line of his firm lips, and her own began to tingle as she imagined the feel and the taste of him. She swayed toward him, an invitation he was quick to take advantage of.

His hands cupped her soft buttocks, lifting her into the cradle of his hips.

Willingly she went, allowing him to crush her soft curves against his lean hardness.

A startled gasp escaped her as he lightly nipped her lower lip between his strong teeth. Her mouth parted, and his tongue thrust inside, scraping abrasively against hers.

For a brief second she tried to retreat, but his hand held her head immobile as he explored the moist softness. An exquisite sensation of euphoria bubbled through her, and Jenny lost both her momentary fear and her inhibitions, pressing herself closer to him.

"What are you doing to Jenny?" Jed's shrill voice sliced through the haze of passion clouding her mind, and she went rigid.

Slowly Nick raised his head and glared at the small boy standing in the doorway. "When a door is closed, you knock and wait for permission before entering," he growled.

"You let go of my Jenny!"

"Jed," Jenny began soothingly.

"Either close that door as you leave, or you're going to get what you should have gotten years ago, a good spanking!"

"Nick, that's enough." Jenny hastily stepped back and nervously rubbed her hands over her thighs. She felt as if she'd been caught in a monumental indiscretion, which she knew was ridiculous. She had a right to kiss her own husband. So why did she feel so disloyal? Because she'd been so engrossed in Nick's embrace that she'd not only forgotten Jed, but also she'd actually resented it when he'd burst in on them. A confusing mixture of frustration, anger and guilt filled her.

"That kid—" Nick began.

"*Jed!* His name is Jed," she snapped, "and he didn't know—"

"Oh, I think the kid knew quite well what he was doing."

"He . . ." Jenny began to defend Jed, only to pause as she caught sight of the smug expression on the boy's face. She was being manipulated, she suddenly realized. Jed was cleverly using her to strike at Nick, and she couldn't allow it. Not if there was to be any peace in their home over the next year.

"Nick is right, Jed. You know perfectly well you're not supposed to walk into someone's bedroom without knocking first. For that lapse in manners you owe me an apology." She forced herself to ignore Jed's expression of hurt fury that she would dare to take him to task in front of Nick.

"What he needs—" Nick began ominously.

"I don't believe in physical violence," she stated emphatically, "either by or against children."

"Yeah," Jed jeered, and Jenny came perilously close to forsaking all her principles of child rearing.

"Go to your room, Jed," she ordered.

"But, Jenny—"

"Right this minute. I am so upset and—" Her voice cracked, and Jed looked horrified at her break in composure. "We'll talk later when we've all calmed down. I'm going down to the quilt shop."

Ignoring both of them, she ran out.

6

"WHAT D'YA WANT?" Jed demanded in response to the sharp rap on his closed bedroom door.

"In," Nick replied succinctly.

"Go away. I don't want to talk to you." His voice was thick with suppressed tears.

"I can't say that I'm all that keen to talk to you, either, but I think it's necessary." Nick's voice sharpened with anger. He'd had a long tiring day capped by a frustrating encounter with Jenny that had left him longing to make love to her. A desire that had been thwarted because of the spoiled brat on the other side of this door. A spoiled brat who was about to be told a few home truths about his behavior.

Nick pushed the door open and stalked into the room. Jed was huddled in a tight ball on his bed.

"You . . . Dammit, look at me when I talk to you!"

"Why? Do you do tricks?" Jed rolled over and glared sullenly at him.

Despite his anger, Nick was moved at the naked misery in the boy's face. Jed's behavior might have upset Jenny, but he clearly hadn't derived any pleasure from doing it.

Nick walked over to the window and stared down at the shop's parking lot below. Now what? he asked himself in exasperation. He'd come in here intending to read the kid the riot act, but he found he couldn't. Yelling at Jed would be like kicking a puppy. But something had to be done. Jenny's frantic expression as she'd rushed out of the apartment was proof of that.

Taking a deep breath, Nick sat down beside the boy. Jed, with a look of intense dislike, scooted away.

"Listen, kid . . . Jed," he corrected himself. "I know you don't like me—"

"What was your first clue, Sherlock?" Jed sneered.

"And, conversely, you don't make the list of my ten favorite people."

"You don't like me?" Jed's eyes widened as he considered an idea that had obviously never occurred to him before.

"Can you give me one good reason why I should? You've behaved like a spoiled brat from the first moment I saw you."

"A brat!"

"A spoiled brat. Actually, you aren't much of an advertisement for Jenny's skill as a mother."

"What!"

"From what I know about Jenny, I'd have expected her to have taught you better manners."

"What do you know about Jenny?"

Not as much as I wish I did, Nick thought with a flash of humor. "A lot more than you do, ki—Jed. It was because of your Jenny that I got one of the few spankings of my life."

"Oh?" Jed asked cautiously.

"Uh-huh, when I was about your age. Jenny and my sister, Angie, were the bane of my life. They used to follow me everywhere. One day they kept demanding that I pull them in Angie's wagon, but I wanted to play baseball."

"Yeah?"

"When I wouldn't, they sat on second base and wouldn't go home. Have you ever tried to play ball with a pair of girls hugging the base and screaming if you tried to slide?"

"That doesn't sound like my Jenny," he muttered. "She understands how important baseball is."

"But it is Jenny. Or, more accurately, it was. Somehow, I can't see the Jenny of today sitting on a base and refusing to move. Now it's her son who's doing it."

"I never did!"

"Figuratively speaking, that's exactly what you've been doing," Nick was careful to keep his voice nonjudgmental. "You've taken the stand that you hate me and you refuse to budge from it. Despite what Jenny wants."

"Jenny doesn't want you!" Jed glared at him. "She only married you because we needed a dad in our family so's she could adopt me!" Jed used his suspicions as a weapon.

Nick stared at him in exasperation. Everything would be so much simpler if they could just tell the kid that their marriage was only going to last for a year. But Jenny was undoubtedly right. Jed would tell a friend, and within a week the whole town would know, which would defeat the purpose of their getting married in the first place. No, Jed had to believe that theirs was a normal marriage.

"The added pressure from Social Services certainly speeded things up," Nick said. "Originally, I'd planned to stay in the Middle East for another year before I asked Jenny to marry me."

"I don't believe you." Jed sounded unsure of himself.

"What don't you believe? That I've wanted to marry Jenny for years? Doesn't it strike you as odd that I should suddenly appear just when Jenny needed a husband?"

"It was a coincidence," Jed insisted.

"Nope, it was good planning. Jenny mentioned the problem in her last letter, and I hurried home."

"But you said you didn't want any babies." Jed sounded confused.

"Well, you aren't all that much of an advertisement for kids," Nick snapped and was immediately ashamed of himself.

"I guess I'm not, am I?" Jed's honest admission gave Nick a brief glimpse of the boy Jenny loved.

"No," Nick agreed. "But I shouldn't have said so. That was a low blow. I'm sorry."

"S'okay." Jed shrugged and then glanced sideways at Nick. "But I still don't like you."

"Is it necessary that you do? Listen, Jed, your behavior isn't hurting me because I don't care enough about you to be hurt. The person you're hurting is Jenny."

"I know." Jed began to trace the seam line of his colorful quilt with a grubby finger.

"Suppose we were to call a truce?"

"A truce? You mean I should pretend to like you?"

"No, pretending to tolerate me will suffice. And, in exchange, I'll tolerate you. We may not like each other, but we both like Jenny. So why don't we think of her instead of our own feelings?"

"What exactly do I have to do?" Jed asked suspiciously.

"Treat me like a guest, and if you find that you can't contain your dislike of me, wait until Jenny is out of hearing before you say anything. Agreed?" Nick held out his hand, and to his relief Jed shook it.

"Agreed."

"Now that that's settled, why don't we go pick up a pizza for supper. I doubt if Jenny will feel like cooking tonight."

"Can we go in your Corvette?" He scooted off the bed. "Sure."

"Nick, would . . ." Jed took a deep breath. "Would you teach me to drive your car?"

"No," Nick said flatly.

"But, Nick." Jed clattered down the stairs after him. "It's legal for me to drive on private property, and there's lots of private property on your farm."

"Never share either your woman or your Corvette with another man."

"I'm not a man. I'm just a little boy," Jed said triumphantly.

"With all the instincts of a corporate lawyer." Nick climbed into the car.

"Thank you." Jed scrambled in after him.

Nick turned on the ignition. "Buckle your seat belt."

"We're only going three blocks."

"No seat belt, no ride. The choice is yours."

"You're as bad as Jenny," Jed grumbled as he fastened the belt.

Nick put the car in First and pulled out of the parking lot, faintly surprised that Jed had given in so easily. He glanced speculatively at the boy, who was madly waving to a friend to make sure he noticed the car he was riding in. Nick's lips twitched at the envious expression on the other boy's face. It was a good thing the Corvette had only two seats, or he'd have found himself pestered to death to give rides to all of Jed's friends.

"I'LL HELP JENNY with the dishes." Jed stared at Nick, who had no trouble interpreting the message. Jed wanted to be alone with her. It was a sentiment Nick could sympathize with. He'd like to get her alone, too. Tomorrow, he promised himself. She ate lunch alone in the flat at one, and Jed didn't get home from school until after three. That gave him a good two hours. And they would be good, too. He felt a wave of anticipation flood him.

"Okay?" Jed asked.

"Thanks, Jed. I wanted to watch the news."

Thoughtfully Jenny watched Nick leave. He had called Jed by his given name instead of "kid." Did it mean anything? She picked up the remains of the pizza and started toward the kitchen. What had happened between them this afternoon after she'd left? She wasn't left wondering for long.

"Jenny. . ." Jed handed her a dirty plate to put in the dishwasher.

"Hmm?" she murmured encouragingly.

"I'm sorry I went into your bedroom without knocking," he muttered. "I won't do it again."

"Thank you. I'd appreciate that."

"And I won't be nasty to Nick no more."

"Anymore. Does that mean you like him now?"

"No. It means that we're going to try to tolerate each other because even if we don't like each other, we both like you," he quoted Nick. "And—"

"Damn!" Nick's sharply bitten-off expletive was followed by the sound of something breaking.

Jenny hurried into the living room to find Nick sitting on the sofa, a broken mug on the floor at his feet and hot coffee running down his arm onto the carpet. His face had hardened into sharp lines, and beneath his tan his skin had a pasty hue.

"What's wrong, Nick?" Jenny looked at the television screen he was staring at. A dead man was being loaded into an ambulance.

"That's the Middle East?" She hazarded a guess based on the faces and clothing of the people in the picture.

"Lebanon. The bastards murdered him!"

"Did you know the victim?" she asked softly.

"No."

Then why the violent reaction to his death? Jenny wondered. Anyone would feel anger and impotent frustration, but Nick's reaction went beyond that. Far beyond. But why? She didn't know, and at the moment she had no intention of trying to find out. She wanted to erase the bleak expression from his face, not cause him to dwell on it. "Come into the bath and let me put some antiseptic on your hand. This seems to be your day for wounds." She tried to lighten his mood.

"Jed, finish loading the dishwasher, please," she told the wide-eyed boy. "Come on, Nick." Purposefully she moved toward the bathroom.

Filling the bathroom sink with warm water, she stirred in disinfectant and then plunged his hand into it. "Hurt?" She noticed his wince.

"Not really. It's only a scratch."

Jenny peered down at his palm. "You're right. You're also very lucky you were holding a pottery mug instead of some of my china. You could have sliced a tendon."

A sharp rap on the bathroom door claimed their attention.

"Come in, Jed. That is, if you can find the room." Jenny squeezed out of the way as the door opened.

"It's the phone. For him." Jed nodded toward Nick.

"Get a name and tell them I'll call back later," Nick said.

"I already got a name. Adelaide Witton."

"Wait a minute." Nick shook the water off his hand and then hastily dried it on his shirt. "I'll take the call." He squeezed out past Jenny and hurried into the living room.

"Who's Adelaide Witton?" Jed asked Jenny.

"A friend of Nick's," Jenny improvised.

"A girlfriend!" He was clearly outraged.

Jenny tried to ignore the sinking feeling Jed's words caused. "Well, if she's his friend and she's also a girl, then I guess you could call her a girlfriend. Now let's go finish up the dishes, my lad."

"But—" He glanced furtively toward the living room.

"Now. It's extremely rude to eavesdrop." *No matter what the temptation*, she told herself as she tried to block out the comforting murmurs Nick was making into the phone.

"GOT A TRUNK HERE for a Nick Carlton." The delivery man stuck his head in the quilt shop.

Jenny felt a sharp stab of excitement. It had to be Nick's belongings from the Middle East. "It goes upstairs. Just leave it in the living room."

"Upstairs! Lady, do you have any idea how heavy that thing is?"

"Would you take it up if I included a tip?"

"Not even if you bought me a truss for the hernia I'd get doing it."

"Then put it in the back room." She gestured behind her.

"As long as there's no steps," he grunted and shoved the bill of lading at her.

"And that's the company that advertises its service." A middle-aged customer shook her head in disgust.

"You know what they say. Always advertise your weakness. Now, what may I do for you?"

"I want to make a log cabin quilt, but I'm not so sure about how to match the colors," she confessed.

"I'll help." Jenny smiled encouragingly. "What do you want as your main color?"

"Dark green to match the rug in my guest room."

"Then let's look over here." Jenny led the woman over to the racks of green material, suppressing her intense curiosity about the trunk being wheeled past her. "When you've decided which of these colors you prefer, we'll discuss accent colors."

"Accent colors!"

"Don't worry," Jenny soothed, pausing as she caught an echo of Nick's encouraging murmurs to Adelaide in her own voice. Was his relationship with Adelaide as easily explained, and if it was, then why didn't he? *Because he probably doesn't think that it's any of your business*, she answered herself. And he'd be right. Their agreement hadn't included a rundown of their past lives, she reminded herself.

After Marge left for lunch, Jenny wandered through the empty shop to the back room and stood studying the battered black trunk. She tried to pick up one end, but it didn't budge. The delivery man hadn't been exaggerating. The only way they were going to get it upstairs was empty. She opened the dirty manila envelope taped to the top, found the key and inserted it in the lock. It turned easily.

A wife should help her husband unpack, she rationalized her behavior. And he hadn't told her not to. Surely if there was anything in the trunk he didn't want her to see, he'd have had it delivered to the farm.

Jenny lifted the lid, wrinkling her nose as the aroma of sandalwood wafted out. She sniffed cautiously. It smelled . . . mysterious. She took some empty cardboard boxes out of the storage room and began to fill them with the contents of the trunk, intending to carry the lighter boxes upstairs. It wasn't until she had almost finished unpacking that she found anything of interest. On the bottom of the trunk was a shoe-box-size container.

Picking it up, she ran her fingertips over the intricately patterned mosaic lid and then, unable to resist the temptation, opened it.

A plastic ID badge with a picture of Nick was sitting on top of a pile of papers. She picked it up, frowning as she took in the details of the uniform he was wearing. It wasn't one she recognized. A chill feathered over her skin. What was Nick doing wearing some strange uniform? Hastily she placed the badge to one side and dug farther into the box.

It was filled with papers, all in an incomprehensible language that she suspected was Arabic.

"What are you doing?"

Jenny jumped guiltily at the unexpected sound of Nick's voice. "Nick! You scared me half to death."

"Why aren't you in the shop? Anyone could have walked off with the contents of your cash drawer."

"The register's locked." Jenny eyed him warily, trying to gauge his reaction to having caught her snooping. "Your trunk was delivered this morning, and I was unpacking it for you. I found this box." She held it out. "I'm sorry if it's a secret."

"If it were a secret, I'd hardly have put it where any customs agent could find it."

"Nick, why were you wearing a uniform?"

"Free laundry went with the job."

"But what job?"

He studied her worried face for a few seconds. "After leaving the navy I set up an intelligence-gathering unit for the emirate of Abar and ran it for a few years before going into the business of selling and servicing oil-drilling equipment."

"You were a spy?" she asked incredulously.

"Hardly," Nick said dryly. "I simply gathered and collated information on everything from the price of airline tickets to which greengrocer the Soviet embassy patronized."

"Oh." Jenny chewed her lip. Her gut feeling was that there was more to what he'd done than what he was admitting to, but perhaps his memories weren't pleasant ones. She remembered his extreme reaction to the newscast. If so, she had no intention of badgering him about them.

Changing the subject, she said, "Marge'll be back from her lunch in a few minutes. How about if I fix us something to eat then?"

"Thanks, I'll grab a quick shower while I'm waiting. I cleaned out the bottom floor of the barn this morning and I smell like it. And don't try to lug those boxes upstairs, Jenny. I'll do it later."

He sprinted up the back steps, a rueful curve twisting his lips at her vision of him as another James Bond. The prime requisite for spying was the ability to blend into a crowd, and at six-four and with blue eyes he'd never have stood a chance of passing unnoticed anywhere in the Middle East.

Nick paused as he crossed the living room, his eyes going to the phone. It was over a week since he'd talked to Murad. It wouldn't hurt to check on the negotiations. He punched in a string of numbers and waited until he was connected.

"Murad? Nick here. How's it going?"

"Perfectly." Murad chuckled. "They can hardly believe their luck that we're actually willing to trade so many terrorists for one insignificant businessman."

"What kind of time frame are we talking about?"

"Possibly six to eight weeks. I've found out a little more about the group we're dealing with."

"Such as?"

"Mostly names and backgrounds. It appears that we're holding the younger brother of one of the leaders of the group, and their mama is putting pressure on her eldest to get her baby boy out of our nasty jail."

"It's hard to believe those bastards have mothers that love them."

"Speaking of families, how's Witton's wife doing?"

"She seems calmer since I told her that things were progressing so well and that we'd have Don home by Thanksgiving."

"That we *hope* to have Don home for Thanksgiving," Murad corrected. "Nothing is definite when one's dealing with a bunch of fanatics."

"He's got to be home in time for his child's birth." Nick's words were emphatic.

"*Inshallah*," Murad intoned. "I'll keep you posted."

"Thanks, I'd appreciate it."

Nick hung up the phone with a feeling of lightheartedness. Everything was working out. Murad was going to gain Witton's freedom, leaving Nick free to plan his own future.

"The Ladies' Bazaar has a great sale on wool skirts," Marge said as she hurried into the shop.

"I'll check it out later, Marge," Jenny called over her shoulder as she hurried upstairs, her mind on Nick. This was the first time he'd returned to the flat for lunch. Why had he varied his schedule today? Because he'd known that the trunk would be arriving and wanted to be around if she pried? But she had, and he hadn't seemed angry. She frowned, trying to identify his reaction. He'd seemed more amused than anything at her assumption that he'd been a spy.

Jenny paused in the living room, listening for the sound of the shower. The flat was silent.

"Nick?" she called. "What do you want for lunch?"

"Mummpf." His muffled voice came from the bedroom.

"Sorry, I'm fresh out of mummpf." She walked into the bedroom to find Nick rummaging through a bureau drawer. A pale blue towel was wrapped around his lean hips, and his broad shoulders glistened with water droplets.

Jenny swallowed uneasily as a feeling of claustrophobia pressed down on her. Nick represented too much untrammeled masculinity for her small bedroom to contain. It wasn't exactly the towel he was wearing, she thought, trying to analyze her reaction in an attempt to neutralize it. She saw men at the YMCA pool wearing a lot less every time she swam and she barely noticed them. Perhaps it was the intimacy of the situation, she considered. Just the two of them. Alone. In her bedroom. It didn't matter what it was. She could handle it, she encouraged herself. Taking a deep breath, she straightened her shoulders and tried for a nonchalant approach.

"What do you want for lunch, Nick?" She hoped he hadn't noticed the unexpectedly husky timbre of her voice.

"You," he said calmly, continuing to rummage through the drawer. "Where did you put my socks?"

"One drawer down." She stared uncertainly at his dark head. Had he really said that, or had she simply heard an echo of her own desire?

"Well?" Nick extracted a pair of socks and tossed them on the chair.

"Well what?" Her voice cracked, and she closed her eyes in self-disgust. So much for the nonchalant approach.

"Shy, Jenny?" His deep voice was threaded with humor.

"I'm not shy." She opened her eyes to find Nick standing directly in front of her. "At least, not much," she mumbled, disconcerted by the hot glow of desire burning deep in his bright blue eyes. It was so long since a man had looked at her with such need, and she found it a heady feeling.

"There's no reason to be shy of me, Jenny." He cupped her cheek and ran his thumb over her bottom lip, learning its soft texture.

Jenny gasped at the tingling sensation that spread from his caressing movement. Her heartbeat accelerated, and she

ignored an instinctive impulse to retreat. She might be a little shy, but she certainly wasn't afraid of either Nick or what
he was promising.

His thumb parted her lips, and the slightly salty taste of
his finger flooded her mouth. His large hand cupped the
back of her neck, urging her forward.

"Sweet, sweet Jenny," he murmured. "You smell like a
flower garden. An old-fashioned flower garden full of unexpected delights." Lightly he brushed his mouth back and
forth across her lips, and she muttered protestingly, wanting him to deepen his insubstantial caress.

Jenny wiggled closer to his heat-laden body. She sighed
with pleasure as he began to nibble on her lower lip, alter-
nately nipping and soothing with darting strokes of his
tongue. He slipped his hand beneath her sweater, and Jenny
shuddered at the feel of his work-roughened fingers as they
inched their way up over her rib cage. She tensed in anticipation as his hand hovered above one of her small lace-
covered breasts. Cupping the soft mound, he slowly rubbed
his thumb back and forth across the hardening tip.

A sensation of vertigo shook her as he swiftly disposed
of both her sweater and bra, negligently tossing them aside.

"How beautiful you are, Jenny." His thickened voice
fanned her excitement. "You feel like velvet." He caught the
dark pink nipple between his thumb and forefinger and
gently tugged it.

"God! You make me feel so..." He bent her body over his
arm, and his mouth closed greedily over her breast.

Wave upon wave of exquisite sensation radiated from the
heat of his devouring mouth, and she trembled convulsively.

"That's right, Jenny. Give in to it. Let it carry you along."

To where? To drown in the feeling he was arousing, the
rational part of her mind tried to warn her. Her reaction was

going beyond simply enjoying his caresses. Far beyond. She was being swamped by his lovemaking. By the feel of his warm mouth, his probing hands and the pressure of his hard body. Never had she lost control of herself to this extent, and she found it vaguely frightening. Lovemaking was supposed to be a warm, sharing experience with a beloved partner. Not this wildly tempestuous explosion of the senses.

Jenny caught her breath in an audible gasp as she felt the zipper of her jeans give way beneath his fingers, but before her muddled mind could react, he had yanked them down over her slim hips. Scooping her up in his arms, he placed her on the bed and dropped down beside her.

Jenny stared into his face. Passion had sharpened his features, blurring her normal image of him. Nick was totally involved in making love to her, she realized with a growing sense of exultation. He wasn't treating this as a casual encounter. This was important to him. On what level she didn't begin to comprehend, but that didn't matter. What mattered was that he was making love to her as if she were the most important thing in his universe.

She sucked in her breath as he lightly drew his blunt nails over her abdomen, and a quivering started deep inside her. A quivering that escalated into a resonant throbbing as he slowly peeled her lacy briefs off. His mouth followed their downward path, and he paused to thoroughly investigate her soft, scented curves.

"Nick?" Her voice was an incoherent plea that he quickly responded to.

Flinging aside his towel, he nudged her legs apart with his knee and slipped between them.

"We'll have to work on your staying power, Jenny." His unsteady chuckle ricocheted through her whirling mind.

"Is this what you want, my lovely?" He thrust forward with a powerful movement of his hips.

"Yes!" Jenny was beyond pretense. Nothing mattered but that he satisfy the ache he'd created. She wrapped her arms around him and greedily pulled him closer. "Don't stop."

"I couldn't if I wanted to." His words held a wealth of promise. A promise he proceeded to redeem, hurtling Jenny into a world of pure sensation that inundated her mind and spilled over into her receptive body.

Nick held Jenny close for a few moments, then released her slightly to stare down into her flushed face in supreme satisfaction. Her bright red hair was in disarray. Her long brown lashes shadowed her creamy cheeks, and her swollen lips were parted as her breath came in shallow gasps.

"You, madame, are the embodiment of every sensual delight." He dropped a lazy kiss on her small nose. "Practically perfect in every way."

"Only practically?" she murmured, trying to gather the energy to move. The problem was that she didn't really want to. She wanted to hang on to the lingering remnants of the most incredible experience of her life as long as possible.

Lazily his hand cupped one of her soft breasts. "You don't want to be perfect," he said seriously. "The Arabs believe that perfection tempts the fates, so they deliberately put a tiny flaw into anything they make."

Jenny trembled as his callused fingers tugged the sensitized tip.

"Dessert," he suddenly said.

"What?" She blinked at him in confusion.

"Having just wolfed down the main course, I'm now going to indulge in dessert. A long, leisurely dessert," he whispered against her parted lips.

"Wolf is right," Jenny giggled, happily moving to meet him.

7

"SO HOW'S MARRIED LIFE treating you, Jenny?" Sarah Pearson dropped the bolts of fabric she was carrying on the counter. "I need two yards of the dark blue and a quarter of the others."

"Okay." Jenny began measuring them, hoping that Sarah's question was strictly rhetorical. She didn't want even the most casual examination of her marriage. Not after the cataclysmic lovemaking she'd shared with Nick earlier that afternoon. Her feelings toward him were too confused and too unexpected for casual discussion.

"Hey, come on, girl. Wake up." Sarah snapped her fingers in Jenny's face. "Life must be pretty good if just the thought of Nick can send you off into a trance. At least you picked a loyal one."

"Loyal?"

"Hmm, I was in the bank yesterday when Nick was there and Elsie tried to pick him up."

"Pick him up!" Jenny was vaguely surprised by the strength of the outrage that shook her. It was for Jed's sake, she assured herself. They couldn't afford any scandal.

"Bold as brass." Sarah nodded. "I was behind them in line, so I heard every word. She was wearing a pair of ridiculously high heels, and she pretended to trip and grabbed on to Nick. Then she moaned about having wrenched her ankle and she didn't know how she was ever going to get home." Sarah snorted. "That was his cue to say he'd drive her, of course. I was about to offer a lift—"

"Now that's friendship." Jenny grinned.

"How could I do any less for someone I sat next to all through school? But the sacrifice wasn't necessary. Nick told Mrs. Beamish, the teller, to call a taxi. He even paid for it. Apparently pushy blondes don't appeal to him. And speaking of pushy women, I've been meaning to ask you, how does Jed like his new teacher?"

"Margot Harmon? He doesn't. I've been to school twice already, and it's still September. What does Bryan think of her?"

"That she's a stupid cow. But you know Bryan. He's hardly an impartial observer. He'd defend Jed to his dying breath, and if he doesn't get those leaves raked in our backyard, it may come to that." She accepted her sack of material from Jenny. "Thanks, I'll see you later."

"Bye." Jenny slowly replaced the bolts of fabric on the racks while she considered Nick's refusal of Elsie's invitation. Why had he exhibited such a total lack of interest in such a beautiful, sophisticated woman? But maybe Nick, having traveled the world, was well used to beautiful, sophisticated women? The thought brought her no comfort. If it was true, he certainly wasn't going to be overly impressed by her own freckle-faced charms. She grimaced at her reflection in the plate-glass window.

"Hey, Jenny." Marge stuck her head out of the back room. "The junior high school just called, and they want seventy-six two-yard pieces of one hundred percent cotton fabric and enough batting to make seventy-six pairs of oven mitts for the eighth-grade home ec class. Should I start cutting it now?"

"Might as well." Jenny forced her mind back to business. "And Marge, make sure all the pieces are the same print. I sent a variety last year, and it was a big mistake. One of the cheerleaders chose hers first, and half the rest of the girls wanted the same fabric. Why don't you use one of those new Christmas prints we got in last week?"

"Sure." Marge paused and then took a closer look at Jenny. "You okay? You look kind of pale. As a matter of fact, you look a lot pale."

"I'm fine, Marge. Come on, I'll help you cut while we aren't busy." She stifled a sigh. She didn't know about pale, but she was certainly tired. Probably the aftermath of what she and Nick had shared earlier, she thought. It wasn't possible to spend that much emotionally and not feel drained. She'd feel better tomorrow.

BUT CONTRARY TO HER EXPECTATIONS she didn't feel better the next morning. She found it an effort to even drag herself out of bed. She labeled her lethargy emotional exhaustion and tried her best to ignore it.

"I said I wanted grape." Jed scowled at the offending glass of orange juice Jenny had just set down in front of him.

"Sorry," she muttered, reaching back into the refrigerator.

"Thanks." Jed accepted the replacement she handed him.

Jenny sipped the rejected orange juice and then grimaced.

"What's the matter?" Nick entered the tiny kitchen, and the force field of energy that seemed to surround him danced over her skin, momentarily investing her with a spark of energy.

"It tastes bitter."

Nick took the glass out of her hands, tasted it and then frowned at her. "It seems all right to me." He placed the back of his hand against her milk-white cheek.

Jenny's heart began to beat erratically at his touch. *Play it cool*, she told herself. A task that became much easier as she noticed the malevolent gaze Jed leveled at Nick. But to her relief Jed didn't say anything. He simply began shoveling scrambled eggs into his mouth.

"You're hot," Nick said.

"I've been cooking breakfast." She backed up a step.

"You're still—"

"Don't fuss," she said irritably. "Would you like some eggs?"

"I'll get them. You sit down. What would you like to eat?"

"Nothing." Jenny's stomach squirmed at the very thought of food.

"I told you, you should always eat breakfast. It's the most important meal of the day," Nick reproved.

"That's what I always tell her," Jed spoke up, "but she doesn't listen."

"That's because she's a woman. Women aren't ruled by logic like us men." Nick gave her a sidelong glance, his eyes brimming with laughter. "Women are to be pitied."

"You two are going to be the ones to be pitied because if you don't knock it off, I'm liable to give in to a burst of feminine emotionalism and refuse to cook your supper."

"Jenny!" Jed looked horrified. "You wouldn't starve us, would you?"

"Starve is what you two would do if you were left to your own devices." She eyed them with a jaundiced eye.

"Jenny!" Jed wailed.

"Don't worry." She grimaced. "I don't intend to starve anyone."

"Wise." Nick grinned. "I can think of much more productive ways to utilize a burst of feminine emotionalism."

Jenny frowned quellingly at him. That was not a subject she wanted to explore, especially not around Jed.

"Just to prove our hearts are in the right place, we'll wash the breakfast dishes for you," Nick offered.

"You're on," Jenny eagerly accepted. She didn't mind cooking, but she hated doing dishes. As did Jed. Predictably he began to complain.

"I can't help. I have to catch the bus."

"You've got twenty-five minutes before the school bus comes," Nick countered.

"Since you two—" she fixed Jed with a warning glance "—are doing the dishes, I'm going to get an early start downstairs. Fridays are always hectic, and we still have to finish cutting out the material for the junior high school. See you later."

She gave them a quick smile and beat a hasty retreat to avoid having to listen to Jed's complaints about violations of child labor laws and mental cruelty to his emerging masculine psyche. She let herself into the shop and headed toward the front to open it, hoping her lethargy would wear off.

It didn't. By noon she felt as if she were swimming through Jell-O. She paused in her futile search for another box of white quilting thread and leaned her spinning head against the storeroom wall.

"Why didn't you say you were sick this morning?" Nick demanded, coming in unexpectedly.

"I'm not sick." She lifted her head from the wall with an effort.

"Then you're giving a damn good imitation of it, woman. Come on. It's bed for you." He scooped her up in his arms.

Jenny gasped as the sudden movement sent her head reeling. Her fingers clutched the thin cotton of his shirt, and her head lolled against his chest. The steady, rhythmic beat of his heart echoed in her ears, adding to her sense of disorientation.

"Nick." She made a determined effort to clear her thoughts. "I can't be sick."

"From the looks of you, you couldn't be much sicker." He sprinted up the back stairs to their flat.

"I mean we're too busy on Fridays for me to be sick. And not only that, but I'm supposed to be teaching a class this afternoon on making folded stars for Christmas."

"What about that kid who helped out the day we were married?"

"Letty, and for heaven's sake, don't call her a kid," Jenny protested. "She'd be crushed. She thinks she's all grown-up."

"Only in body." Nick strode through the empty flat. "She hasn't had enough experience with life to be interesting yet."

And what kind of life experience was he referring to? Jenny remembered her earlier doubts. Certainly not the kind gained by running a quilt shop in a tiny town in Up-state New York. She sniffed self-pityingly.

"So what about Letty?" Nick gently put Jenny in the middle of their bed and began to efficiently strip off her clothes, ignoring her ineffectual attempts to stop him. "Can she help Marge?"

"She'll be in as soon as she gets out of school at two-thirty, but even if Marge teaches my class, Letty could never cope with the shop on her own."

"She won't have to." Nick bundled her under the covers. "I'll help."

"You!" Jenny forced herself to sit up.

"Don't move." He left the room to return a few minutes later with two aspirin and a glass of water.

"Take these." He popped the aspirin into her mouth when she opened it to protest.

Jenny swallowed and tried again. "Nick, you can't help out in the shop."

"Why not?"

"Because you're a man and . . ." She fumbled for an answer he'd accept. The real reason she didn't want him in her shop wasn't any too clear, even in her own mind. She just knew that Nick seemed to be infiltrating all areas of her life and she didn't like it. Or, to be more accurate, she liked it too much, she admitted honestly. It would be disastrous if she came to depend on him because he wasn't going to be a permanent fixture in her life.

"So? According to that quilting book of yours I was reading yesterday, Jeffrey Gutcheon is one of the foremost quilting experts in America and he's certainly a man."

"But he's experienced."

"So am I." Nick grinned at her.

"At quilting!"

"Everyone has to start somewhere, and if I'm going to have a wife with a quilt shop, I'd better learn. Besides, all you do is cut material. What could go wrong?"

"I don't even want to think about it." Jenny shuddered.

"Then don't. Just lie back and let the aspirin work while I go help Marge." He pulled the covers up around her chin and patted her comfortingly on the head.

"It's a bad idea," she murmured as she listened to the receding sound of his footsteps. But right then she was incapable of getting up and doing something about it. She'd close her eyes for just a moment and then she'd get up, she decided.

But when she awoke, it was to find the room in twilight and Jed sitting on the end of her bed.

"Hi." She smiled weakly at him. "Don't get too close. I'm probably contagious."

"S'okay," Jed assured her. "I only want to know if you're hungry. Nick let me order a pizza, and I got one with everything on it. You want some?"

"No, thanks." Jenny swallowed uneasily. "I just want to sleep." She closed her eyes again.

"Not yet," Jed yelled, and Jenny winced at the sound. "Nick said you were to drink something if you woke up. There's a glass of orange juice on your bedside table."

"It can stay there," Jenny muttered. "It tastes bitter."

"Not really. The flu is upsetting your sense of taste, so sour tastes bitter. I wonder what sweet would taste like?"

Jenny opened one eye and then closed it at the speculative gleam in his. "Go take your spirit of scientific inquiry somewhere else."

"But no one else is sick," Jed pointed out. "Aren't you the least bit curious?"

"No."

"Well, it's your sense of taste," he conceded, "but you still have to drink something because if you don't, Nick said we have to call the doctor."

"Fine, you go get me a glass of 7-Up." Her eyes closed the minute he left the room.

The next time she opened them, it was broad daylight and Jed's face was six inches from hers.

"Jed, what are you doing?"

"Counting your freckles. Your skin's so white that it makes each of them stand out."

"Go away, you unnatural child."

"Hmm, the health book was right. The flu does make you irritable."

"What a comfort to know I'm following the prescribed pattern. What time is it?"

"Twelve-thirty."

Twelve-thirty! She jackknifed up, wincing as her head started to pound. "How can it be twelve-thirty?"

"Well, the earth rotates," Jed began, taking her question literally.

"Why didn't anybody call me?"

"Because you were sleeping, and the doctor said that was the best thing for you," Marge spoke from the doorway.

"Doctor?"

"I told you if you didn't drink Nick was going to call the doctor," Jed reminded her.

"What I want to know is how he convinced him to make a house call."

"Your husband's a pretty determined man," Marge chuckled. "Here, drink this."

Jenny accepted the glass of 7-Up Marge handed her and set it on the bedside table. "I will, but first, I want to wash my face." Gingerly she climbed out of bed.

"Need any help?" Marge offered.

"No, thanks, but don't go away. I want to talk to you."

"I won't. Take your time."

Five minutes later Jenny crept back into bed, the short trip having left her exhausted.

"Jed's right," Marge observed. "You can count your freckles."

"Cut the comedy and tell me how you coped yesterday."

"I coped fine. However, I'm not so sure about some of our customers."

"Oh, no," Jenny groaned. "Give me the gory details."

"Well, I would say your husband has two faults."

"Only two?"

"He's disgustingly honest and he has no appreciation for quilting. As he explained to Tess Henderson, he thinks it's the height of stupidity to take a large piece of material, cut it up into small pieces and then sew them back into one large piece."

"Rather a sweeping condemnation of a whole art form," Jenny said wryly. "How'd Tess take it?"

"Don't worry. I doubt she even heard him. She was too busy drooling over his body."

"Marge!"

"There's no sense hiding your head in the sand, Jenny," Marge said calmly. "Nick Carlton is a gorgeous hunk of masculinity. Most women are going to look. Especially in a small town like Litton where there isn't that much to look at. It doesn't mean a thing. The time to worry is when he starts to look back, and from what I've seen, he's totally oblivious to all the come-hither looks he's getting."

"Umm." Jenny was surprised at the feeling of relief that surged through her tired body. The relief was on Jed's behalf, she told herself. Jed didn't deserve other kids making cracks about what his stepfather was up to.

"However, you may have to unruffle some feathers about his first fault," Marge said slowly.

"For being honest?"

"Disgustingly honest," Marge corrected. "Although in all fairness to Nick, he probably thought she really wanted to know. I mean, she did ask."

"Apparently asking is the only way to get any information around here. Forget the editorial comments and tell me what happened."

"Well, you know Delcy Carr?"

"Waist-length hair, muddy complexion, pushing forty and dresses like she's still a teenager?"

"That's the one. It seems she's decided to make a quilt that matches her coloring. . . ." Marge paused.

"If you think I'm going to ask why, you've got another think coming. Continue."

"Well, she picked out a whole range of purples—"

"Purples! With her spotty complexion?"

"Purples with chrome-yellow accents."

"Yuck, I always knew that woman's taste was all in her mouth," Jenny muttered.

"Then she sidled up to Nick and asked him how she looked in those colors—"

"And he told her," Jenny said in resignation.

"The plain, unvarnished truth."

Jenny sighed. "Well, one thing's certain. Nick's not cut out to keep shop."

"Not unless it's a bodybuilding place. You should have seen him lifting bolts in the stockroom. He's got muscles in places most men haven't even got places. What's he been doing in the Middle East all these years?"

Jenny paled even more as all her half-formed fears about Nick's past engulfed her.

"Oh, dear." Marge shot to her feet. "I didn't mean to worry you about the shop. Don't worry. I'll handle it. You just get better," she ordered as she started toward the door.

"I should be back Monday," Jenny called after her.

Nick caught Jenny's words as he strode into the bedroom. "We'll see about Monday on Monday." He eyed her critically. "You look like skim milk." He sat down on the bed and picked up her limp hand. She let it lie in his hard, callused palm. In some curious way she seemed to be absorbing some of the vibrant energy that was so much a part of his personality.

"You need some nourishment."

"Such as?" she asked cautiously, remembering last night's pizza.

"Warm consommé followed by Jello-O. If that stays down, you can try a poached egg and some dry toast."

"Sounds okay, I—" The phone rang, and she automatically reached out to answer it. "Hello."

"Um, I'm sorry to bother you," a feminine voice said hesitantly. "If Nick isn't busy, could I please talk to him? But if he is busy, I could call him later." Adelaide. Jenny recognized the voice.

"No, he's right here, Adelaide." Jenny handed the phone to Nick and then leaned back against the pillows and frankly eavesdropped. Unfortunately, it only left her more confused. From what she was able to figure out from Nick's end of the conversation, someone named Don wanted to buy a hotel on the Oregon coast and his option was about to expire, and Adelaide wanted to know what to do about it.

"I'll call the realtor this afternoon. Don't worry, Adelaide. Don isn't going to lose his hotel," he soothed. "Just leave everything to me. It's no problem. It's the least I can do. Yes, I know. You take care. Goodbye."

Nick hung up and turned to find himself the focus of Jenny's inquisitive gaze.

Damn, he swore silently. She'd been so quiet he'd thought she'd gone back to sleep.

"Nick?" she began.

"How about that consommé?" He tried to sidetrack her.

"How about telling me what's going on? I know our contract doesn't give me the right to ask, but—"

"To hell with that damn contract!" Nick snapped. After what they'd shared yesterday, their relationship had progressed far beyond the sterile limits of their original agreement. And unless Jenny was being willfully blind, she had to know it.

"Please, Nick, it isn't that I don't trust you. It's just that..."

"You've got a lot more imagination than is good for you."

"And what I'm imagining is probably worse than the truth."

He studied her pale features for a few seconds and then, seeming to reach a decision, said, "I didn't tell you about Adelaide when she first called because I didn't want to worry you about a problem that was almost solved. And because I didn't want you to think badly of me for having caused it in the first place," he added honestly. "What is it you want to know?"

"Who's Adelaide, and why does she keep phoning you?"

"Adelaide Witton is the wife of Don Witton, who was my assistant in the Middle East. But she wasn't supposed to be."

"His wife?" Jenny grabbed a loose end of information and followed it.

"Yes. You see, when the political situation in the Middle East began to deteriorate so badly, it was decided to send all the married personnel home and to sell the business to a Saudi concern. In the end only Don and I were left to complete the transfer of ownership. At the time I thought he was single.

"Anyway, one of the last things to be done was for me to show the Saudi company's representative around a remote drilling site in the desert. But the day we were to go, I got sick, so Don went in my place."

"Predictable, since he was the only other one there," Jenny observed when he fell silent.

"What wasn't predictable was that terrorists kidnapped him."

"Why did they want him?"

"They didn't. They wanted me. I sent Don straight into a trap."

"Did you know it was a trap?"

"Hell, no!"

"Then it can hardly be your fault that Don got kidnapped."

"But it was," Nick insisted. "If I hadn't been passing information along to Murad about the terrorist activity I noticed in my travels throughout the Middle East, they would never have been after me."

"You mean you really were a spy?" Her eyes widened.

"No! I was a businessman, and as such I was vitally concerned about the economic and political stability of the region. Terrorism is bad for business."

"I can imagine, but who's Murad?"

"A younger son of the ruling prince of the emirate of Abar. Murad's the head of security and a very good friend of mine."

"Security?" Jenny remembered the picture of Nick in the strange uniform. "And you worked with him once?"

"Not exactly. When I quit to go into business, Murad took over."

"I see," she said slowly. "So where does Murad fit into Witton's kidnapping?"

"The terrorist group demanded the release of fifty of their members from Abarian jails as the price of Don's freedom."

"And Murad refused?"

"It wasn't his decision to make. It was his father's and he agreed to release forty-eight of the fifty. Murad's doing the negotiating.

"That's why I came back to the States when I did. Murad felt that it would be easier to reach some kind of an agreement with the terrorists if I weren't on the scene since I was the one they really wanted. As long as the terrorists thought there was a chance they could use Don to get to me, they wouldn't agree to anything."

"So you came back to tell Adelaide?"

"Not exactly. After the kidnapping, I went through Don's personal papers to try to find his parents' address, and instead, I found his last letter to her. They'd gotten married on his leave last spring and kept the marriage a secret so that he could finish up his contract because he'd been promised a big bonus when the sale went through."

"So you looked up Adelaide?"

"And found her very pregnant." Nick began to pace agitatedly in the small bedroom. "And I had to tell her that the baby's father might never come back and it was all my fault."

"Your getting sick was pure chance, but if you're determined to assign guilt, Witton has to take his share. He knew the rules against married personnel being over there, yet he ignored them. And for what? Money. Hardly the most praiseworthy of motives."

"But Don didn't know all the facts when he made his decision to return to the Middle East. He had no idea that I'd been passing information along to Murad. If he had, he would have realized the dangers of the situation."

"But—"

"No, Jenny. I've been through it all so many times." His voice was bleak. "The cause of everything was my passing along information. All Don and Adelaide's problems stem from that. I did it. It's up to me to fix it."

"Rambo is fiction, my friend." She felt a chill feather through her at his words.

"I know." Nick gave her a lopsided grin. "However, in this case it appears that Murad's skill at the bargaining table will be an adequate substitute."

As long as you aren't the substitute, Jenny thought uneasily, remembering his unequivocal statement that it was all his fault. Nick had a very well developed sense of responsibility. Hadn't she herself used it to nudge him into rescuing her from a situation that could in no way be considered his fault? How much more might he do for Adelaide, whom he considered to be the victim of his own carelessness? A brief flare of panic filled her mind, but she resolutely beat it out. Her agreement with Nick was short-term. His long-range plans were none of her business, she tried to tell herself, but she was finding it harder and harder to believe with every passing day.

"Hey, Nick." Jed burst into the room. "What language is this paper I found on your desk written in?" He waved it at Nick.

"Arabic."

"Neat! Would you teach me to speak it?" Jed asked, his face glowing with enthusiasm.

"I don't see why not. A sharp kid like you could pick it up in no time." Nick smiled at him.

"You could teach me when you're showing me how to drive your Corvette," Jed suggested craftily.

"You'll drive that monstrosity over my dead body," Jenny said flatly.

"That makes our reaction unanimous," Nick said.

"You could at least teach me to drive a tractor." Jed decided to scale down his aspirations a bit. "Farm kids my age drive."

"You live in town," Jenny pointed out.

"But he has a farm—" Jed nodded at Nick "—and you did marry him."

"Yes, but—" Jenny began.

"When I get a tractor, I'll teach you to drive it," Nick promised.

"Gee, thanks, Nick." Jed's eyes gleamed with pleasure.

"Nick, tractors are dangerous!" she objected.

"Everything's dangerous when it's used improperly. Don't worry. I'll teach him safety. Why don't you just lie back while I get you some consommé. Then you can sleep the rest of the night."

"The rest of the night?" Jed's dismayed voice caused her eyes to fly open.

"What's . . . Oh, no!" She groaned. "Tonight's the parents' planning meeting for the Cub Scout camping trip next weekend. Don't worry, Jed, I'll be there."

"No, you won't," Nick objected.

"You don't understand, Nick," Jenny said. "If a parent doesn't show up, the child can't go."

"But you're sick."

"Mr. Spaulding doesn't make exceptions."

"Spaulding?" Nick queried.

"Our leader," Jed supplied.

"He's rather rigid." Jenny massively understated the case. "But since no other father could or would take the troop..."

"From the sound of things, Spaulding takes advantage of the fact," Nick said dryly. "Is there any reason I can't go in your place?"

"Well..." She was sorely tempted to accept his offer. The very thought of getting dressed and going out made her head swim, but she doubted that even the longed-for camping trip was sufficient incentive to make Jed claim Nick as a parent in front of his friends.

"It's settled, then. Right, Jed?" Nick shot a warning look at him.

"Jed, if you'd rather—" Jenny began.

"Of course I'd rather you went, Jenny," Jed said. "But he's right. You shouldn't go anywhere. Don't worry about it. It'll be okay, and we can drive the Corvette to the meeting, can't we?" He peered hopefully at Nick.

"*I* can drive the Corvette. Come on, let's go get your mother something to eat."

Jenny watched them leave with a feeling of contentment. At least one thing was working out. Jed was sticking to his promise to tolerate Nick. Whether his resolve would last remained to be seen, but for now life was much pleasanter than it had been.

IT WAS THE THUD of Jed's sneakers on the outside steps that alerted her to their return three hours later. She put the book she'd been trying to read on the end table beside the couch and looked up.

"What are you doing out of bed?" Nick demanded.

"I wanted a change of scenery. What's wrong?" She glanced from Nick's harassed features to Jed's tense face. The boy looked as if he was about to burst into tears.

Nick ran his hand through his hair, and Jenny clenched her fingers as she remembered its silken texture. Trying to ignore what she told herself was a totally inappropriate feeling, she repeated, "What's wrong?"

"I knew I shouldn't have taken him," Jed burst out and then, with a look of burning anger at Nick, fled to his room, slamming the door behind him.

"Would you please tell me what happened?" Jenny demanded.

"I ran out of cheeks."

"Ran out of cheeks?" she repeated blankly.

"To absorb insults. That little egomaniac . . ." Nick sputtered to a halt.

Jenny closed her eyes in dismay. "You didn't tell him that, did you?" she asked without much hope.

"Among other things. And I'm not sorry. The man was impossible. When we got there, I thought I was going to have to produce a doctor's certificate to prove you really were sick. He seemed to feel you'd caught the flu simply to annoy him. It was all downhill from there."

"With you giving as good as you got," Jenny guessed shrewdly.

"Well, he did say that if we didn't like the way he was running things to speak up." Nick smiled at the memory. "Talk about leading with his chin."

"I'm more concerned with your tendency to lead with your mouth! I take it he refused to take the boys camping?"

"Unless a suitably abject apology is forthcoming."

"Apology?" Jenny latched on to the word.

"Forget it, Jenny. I wouldn't knuckle under to that...that tin-plated dictator for—"

"Why not? You were the one who blew it. Now it's up to you to apologize, unless..." She eyed him consideringly. "Weren't you a Scout?"

"Eagle."

"Then you can take over the troop, starting with this trip."

"What!" Nick yelped. "I haven't taken kids camping since I assisted with a Cub Scout troop when I was working on my Eagle ranking in high school."

"This has nothing to do with experience, recent or otherwise," Jenny insisted. "This has to do with responsibility. You alienated the old leader. You refuse to apologize. So you take the boys camping."

Nick glared at her in impotent frustration, but Jenny refused to relent.

"All right. I'll take them, if you'll come along." He gave her a crafty smile that made her wince. Trust Nick to find her weak point. She'd never been camping in her life. Nor wanted to. Her idea of roughing it was staying in a motel with a black-and-white TV.

"Well?" Nick eyed her smugly.

The desire to wipe the triumphant expression off his face was irresistible.

"I'll do it."

8

"GOOD AFTERNOON, Mrs. Murray, may I help you?" Jenny watched the elderly woman peer furtively around the busy shop.

"Is he here?" Mrs. Murray hissed.

"He?" Jenny frowned. "He who?"

"Nick Carlton. He was here last Saturday when I came in and he was rude." She glared at Jenny. "Very rude. But what can you expect? I remember his grandfather."

"You're one up on me," Jenny said cheerfully, "because I don't."

"Always rude. Called me a stupid flea-brain just because I misspelled a word and lost the spelling bee for our sixth-grade team."

"Sixth grade!" Jenny repeated incredulously.

"I don't doubt you're shocked." Mrs. Murray nodded.

What shocks me is that anyone could hold a grudge that long, Jenny thought wryly. "Perhaps it's time to forget about it," Jenny suggested. "The poor man's been dead thirty years. He's long since gone to his reward."

"Or his punishment," Mrs. Murray suggested darkly.

"Nonetheless, it's over."

"Not as long as his grandson is still insulting me. When I asked him if he liked the material I'd picked out for my new quilt, he said he didn't!" She sniffed. "I've a good mind to take my business elsewhere."

Jenny opened her mouth to tell her to do so in no uncertain terms, then paused as her heart softened with pity. Mrs.

Murray was a very old, very lonely woman who'd out-lived all of her family and most of her contemporaries. It wouldn't hurt to cater to her.

"I hope you won't feel obligated to make the long drive into Elmira or Binghamton," Jenny said. "I know I'd miss seeing you."

"Well . . ."

"And I'm sure Nick didn't mean to upset you. He probably only likes one color."

"My husband, Gerald, was like that. All he ever wanted me to wear was blue. I haven't thought about that in years. Maybe I ought to make a blue quilt," she mused.

"We have a wide selection of blue fabric." Jenny pointed to the racks behind her. "You might check the new bolts that came in a few weeks back from Gutcheon's."

"Well . . ." Mrs. Murray wavered. "Is Nick going to be helping you much in the store?"

"Oh, no, normally he's busy out at the farm. He only helped last weekend because I had the flu."

"You still look a little pale." Sarah Pearson dropped a bolt on the counter. "Give me two and three-quarter yards, please. That is, if you're through, Mrs. Murray?"

With a mutter about the rudeness of the younger generation Mrs. Murray stalked toward the blue fabrics.

"Whew! What upset her?" Sarah asked.

"My esteemed husband."

"Ah." Sarah grinned. "Now *that* I understand. He'd upset the blood pressure of any woman. You're one lucky lady to have bagged Nick Carlton."

Yes, she had been lucky in her impetuous choice of husbands, Jenny conceded. There was so much more to Nick than met the eye. And as Sarah had said, what did meet the eye was pretty spectacular. If only there weren't this mess with the Wittons hanging over their heads. She grimaced.

"You look pained." Sarah eyed her worriedly. "Are you still feeling sick?"

"Nope, I feel great, which is a good thing because I'm going camping tomorrow."

"You'll love it," Sarah enthused. "We jump in our Winnebago and go whenever we get the chance."

"Any resemblance to the type of camping you do and what we're doing is purely coincidental. Nick and I are taking Jed's Scout troop."

"You poor woman!" Sarah looked at her in horror. "Bryan said something about your going along, but I thought it was just wishful thinking on his part. Maybe you could have a relapse of the flu."

"I considered that, but Nick would just call the doctor."

"Yeah, new husbands do tend to be rather attentive," Sarah conceded. "Maybe it won't be too bad. I mean, look at the bright side. The weather's gorgeous, the leaves are spectacular and no Saturday football games. Just peace and quiet."

And no phone calls from Adelaide, Jenny thought and was immediately ashamed of her selfishness. Poor Adelaide needed Nick, and only a very insecure woman could possibly be jealous of the attention he gave her, Jenny lectured herself. Unfortunately, the nature of the bargain she and Nick had struck did not make for feelings of security. She sighed.

"Just tell yourself that you can do anything a nine-year-old can do," Sarah encouraged her.

BUT BY THE NEXT MORNING, Jenny wasn't so sure anyone could keep up with a nine-year-old, let alone a thirty-three-year-old, relatively sedentary woman.

"Sit down and eat your breakfast, Jed." She took another gulp of scalding coffee.

"Speaking of food, you should eat." Nick frowned at her. "Breakfast—"

"Is the most important meal of the day," she finished. "I didn't believe it the first time you said it, and I don't believe it now. Besides, I am getting some nourishment. I put milk in my coffee."

"You know, Jenny, you shouldn't drink so much coffee," Jed mumbled around a mouthful of sausage. "I was reading in *Scientific Quarterly* that too much caffeine predisposes women to osteoporosis. If you aren't careful, you're going to wind up all hunched over."

"Not a chance," Jenny said. "I'll never live long enough to become a little old lady, hunched over or otherwise."

"The life expectancy of the average American woman—" Jed began.

"Jed!" Bryan screamed from the street below. "I'm here."

Jed shoved another sausage in his mouth, grabbed a doughnut and, with a muttered "Excuse me," bolted for the stairs.

"Cheer up, Jenny." Nick cupped her chin in his hard palm and tilted her head back. His thumb moved roughly over the soft skin of her cheek, and Jenny felt prickles of awareness spread from his casual caress. "It shouldn't be too bad."

"In relation to what?" she muttered. "Famine, war?"

"You might even enjoy it." He leaned closer, and Jenny found her attention drawn to the network of fine lines that radiated from the corners of his bright blue eyes. Eyes that were dancing with devilment. "We won't be spending all our time with the boys."

She watched in anticipation as his face descended. His lips rubbed lightly across her parted mouth, and a cascade of shimmering sparks poured through her lips and seeped into her flesh. She felt the tip of his tongue trace along her lower lip, and compulsively, she moved toward him. His hand slipped around her slim waist, pulling her against his hard frame.

Jenny tipped her head back and looked into his eyes, which seethed with emotions, the only one of which she could read with any degree of accuracy was desire. That she had the power to rouse such feeling in a man as experienced as Nick Carlton filled her with a sense of awe.

Slowly, savoring the sensation, she ran her fingertips over Nick's freshly shaved cheek. Tiny pinpricks of sensation flowed up her arm at the raspy texture.

"You feel so—"

"Hungry." He leaned forward, his coffee-flavored breath wafting across her face. "And you are the most tempting morsel on the menu." He gathered her closer, and Jenny willingly went, snuggling into him.

"We're all here, Jenny." Jed clattered up the stairs, and she hastily drew back. Jed's attitude toward Nick, while hardly filial, had been almost cordial this past week. She didn't want to do anything to upset the delicate truce he and Nick had established. Nick's eyes mocked her retreat, but to her relief he made no move to stop her.

"Steve's dad was the last. He's got the troop's equipment in his pickup, and he brought you a present." Jed shoved a brown paper bag at her.

"A present?" Jenny opened the bag and extracted a fifth of whisky. "How nice," she said weakly. "I wonder if he knows something I don't?"

"Alcohol kills brain cells," Jed said, "and you haven't got any to spare."

"I think I proved that by agreeing to come along in the first place," she said, ignoring Nick's muffled laughter.

"No, I just meant that brain cells can't rejuvenate themselves," Jed explained.

"Well, I guess I'm still smart enough to check off our list of camping supplies. Come on, Jed. We'd better get started if we want to reach the campsite by ten."

"We're ready. You're the ones hiding up there."

"Hiding is right," Jenny muttered, watching as Nick picked up the heavy cooler she'd packed. The muscles in his broad shoulders bunched with the effort, and her fingertips tingled as she imagined the feel of them.

"Bring that duffel bag, Jenny," Nick ordered. "And be careful of it. It's fragile."

"Did you think of a bottle, too?" She cautiously hefted it. It weighed almost nothing.

"They don't drink in the Middle East, do they?" Jed held the door for them. "Because of being Muslim?"

"They aren't supposed to drink, but there's often a wide gap between what people are supposed to do and what they actually do."

"There's lots of drug smuggling in the Middle East," Jed said. "Did you know any drug smugglers?"

"Nope." Nick pounded down the stairs. "Most of the smuggling I knew about was guns."

"No wonder they've got so many problems over there," Jenny muttered, trailing along behind them. It was just too bad that they'd had to involve Nick in their disputes. Although she doubted that it had taken much persuasion. She watched Nick load the ice chest into the pickup. Nick had a very strongly developed sense of right and wrong. He'd never ignore a spreading evil. He'd automatically do his best to halt it. But Murad was well on his way to extricating Nick from the consequences of his involvement, she reminded herself. And that being so, there was no reason to spoil a perfectly gorgeous October day worrying about something that was never going to happen. She got into her Caravan, well pleased with life in general.

A feeling that almost lasted through the hour-long trip to the campground. She glanced in her rearview mirror to make sure Nick and Steve's dad were still behind her in the pickup. They were.

"Are we almost there yet, Miss Ryton?" Steve shouted from the back.

"She's not Miss Ryton anymore, you clot," Gordon scoffed. "She married Nick Carlton, so she's Mrs. Carlton."

"I know that," Steve insisted. "I just forgot."

Jenny glanced down at Jed's set features and decided to remove what Jed obviously saw as a grievance.

"Why don't you just call me Jenny, boys?"

"Okay," Steve agreed, "but are we almost there?"

"'Fraid not, Steve. We've still got a good half hour to go."

"Let's sing the bottle song," Bryan yelled.

"Sure," Jed agreed. "How many bottles does it take for half an hour?"

"The bottle of whiskey I left in the flat would have done it," Jenny muttered under her breath.

"A million?" Bryan suggested.

"Nah, ten thousand," Tom said.

"There's ten thousand bottles of beer on the wall, ten thousand bottles of beer," the boys began to sing at the top of their lungs. "If one of those bottles should happen to fall, there'd be nine thousand, nine hundred and ninety-nine bottles of beer on the wall." They took a deep breath and continued, "Nine thousand, nine hundred and ninety-nine . . ."

Jenny gritted her teeth and tried to tune out the singing voices. It proved impossible. By the time she pulled into the parking lot at the campground, her ears rang with the continuous noise and her head was thudding in mute protest.

"It only takes 672 bottles to go half an hour," Jed yelled at Tom.

"That's because you didn't sing fast enough," Tom defended himself. "Wait till we go back."

"Oh, no," Jenny whimpered, tumbling out of the car. Just what she needed. Something to look forward to.

"What's the matter, Jenny?" Nick frowned at her harassed features.

"Daddy, do you know it takes 672 bottles of beer to go a half hour?" Steve jumped out of the Caravan.

"Never drink and drive," his father responded automatically.

"So that's what all that noise was about." Nick's lips twitched.

"Go ahead and laugh, but you're driving them back."

"Not me." Nick solemnly shook his head. "I'm too busy listening to Bill tell me about local farming problems."

"Seriously, Nick." Bill began to hand their equipment down from the bed of his pickup. "Why don't you come along with me to that fruit growers' meeting next week?"

"You ought to," Jenny seconded the idea. "After all, you've got all those apple trees."

"What apple trees?" Nick handed her his duffel bag. "Watch where you put that. It's got the snakebite kit in it."

"Snakebite!" Jenny shot a furtive glance around the graveled parking lot and inched closer to the truck.

"New York State has rattlers," Jed said with pride. "But the Boy Scout Council discourages them in their camps."

"I don't know about the snakes, but I'm already discouraged," Jenny muttered.

"What apple trees?" Nick repeated.

"More than a thousand dwarfs. Your dad planted them just before he died. On the acreage out behind the pasture. Haven't you seen them?"

"I haven't gotten past the outbuildings. I'll take a look next week. Between the deer, the rabbits and the mice, there may not be an orchard left."

"Let me know what you decide." Bill vaulted out of the truck bed. "I'll be back tomorrow at eleven to pick you up."

"Providing there's anything left to pick up," Jenny muttered.

"A Scout is always cheerful," Tom chided her.

"I'm not a Scout, Tom Sinclair. Nor do I have any aspirations to be one."

"You can't, anyway. You're only a girl," Gordon said with a sympathetic glance at her.

"Let's cut out the dissension in the ranks." Nick began handing out the packs. "We'll walk to the campsite. Single file. I'll lead. Jenny, you bring up the rear."

"Yes, sir." The boys happily fell into line.

Twenty minutes later Nick stepped into a small clearing that contained two three-sided shelters with dark green tarps on the fourth sides and one small canvas tent set on a wood platform.

"Where's the lodge?" Jenny looked around the clearing.

"What lodge?" Nick asked.

"When Jed camped here before, they stayed at a lodge on the lake." Jenny eased her pack off.

"Aw, Jenny, that was when I was just a kid," Jed scoffed. "Real men stay in Adirondack shelters. I get the one on the left." He sprinted toward them.

"Put your packs away, boys. And no fighting over the cots," Nick called after them.

"At the risk of repeating myself, I'm not a real man," she said.

"Don't let it worry you, woman. You have everything it takes to appeal to a real man." Nick's eyes gleamed with devilment. "As a matter of fact . . ." His gaze dropped to her small breasts clearly outlined by the green sweater she was wearing.

Jenny felt them tighten with anticipation, but to her disappointment the boys came thundering back before Nick could even kiss her. Ah, well, she consoled herself. Her turn would come. After all, she and Nick would be in the tent, and the boys were going to sleep in the shelters twenty-five feet away. Once they were asleep . . .

"Well?" Nick's indulgent voice intruded on her pleasant daydream.

Jenny looked up to find herself the focus of six pairs of masculine eyes.

"Well, what?" she asked.

"I asked if you would prefer to gather firewood or set up our tent?"

Jenny glanced at the heavy coating of leaves under the trees beyond the camp clearing and shuddered. There could be anything in those leaves: spiders, snakes . . . "I'll do the tent."

"Fine. First, we'll set up. Then we'll go down to the lake and look for animal tracks."

"Great!" Tom voiced the boys' enthusiasm while Jenny kept her opinion of the proposed activity to herself.

Picking up her pack, she carried it over to the tent, lifted the flap and went in. As living quarters it left a lot to be desired. The only furnishings were two single camp cots, which had been pushed up against each other in the middle of the wooden floor.

Purposefully she moved the cots apart, putting Nick's by the door and hers against the back wall. She didn't want Nick to think she was angling for him to make love to her by such a blatant ploy as having the beds together. She had more subtlety than that.

"Here, let me help." Jenny hurried to take one end of the ice chest Nick was pushing through the tent flap.

"Out of the way, woman." He shoved it inside. "Remember, you had the flu last weekend. You don't want to overdo."

"I'm perfectly fine," she insisted.

"I know; otherwise, I'd never have let you come."

"Let me come!" Jenny yelped. "You said if I didn't come, you wouldn't, either."

"So I did." He gave her a thoughtful stare. "Do you suppose my subconscious wants you, too?"

"Too? You mean in addition to your lecherous body?" she quipped.

A gust of anger exploded in his mind. How dare she stick such a derogatory label on what they'd shared. "There's nothing lecherous about my wanting you," Nick bit out. "Our relationship may not be wrapped up in all the tinsel you women call love, but it's honest and it fulfills needs on both sides." He stalked toward the tent flap.

"Nick." Jenny's voice stopped him. "I didn't mean that the way you took it." The sight of his stiff, unbending back forced her to continue. "I only joked about it because I feel confused and uncomfortable and disloyal at the way you make me feel." She bent her head, focusing on a dark brown knot in the pine flooring. "I wasn't trying to put you down."

She watched as his large scuffed Adidas came into her line of vision.

"Why disloyal?" Nick grasped her slender shoulders in his hands and, using his thumb, pushed her chin up.

Embarrassed, Jenny kept her gaze firmly fixed on his square jaw. She hadn't meant to tell him that. It had just slipped out

"Look at me, Jenny," Nick ordered. The force of his personality tugged her gaze upward until it met his. "Tell me why you feel disloyal."

"Because when David touched me, I didn't feel one-tenth of what I do with you and I loved him." Her voice cracked under the strength of her distress. "I did, Nick. I loved David."

A feeling of triumph surged through him. He hadn't been wrong. Jenny had found their lovemaking mind-blowing. Too mind-blowing apparently. He moved to reassure her.

"Of course you did, Jenny." Nick pulled her against him, holding her close. "But the Jenny who loved David is a different person from the Jenny who married me. Just like I'm not the same Nick who used to threaten to beat you to a pulp if you told my mother what I was getting into. Whether we like it or not, time and circumstances change us. You're thirty-three years old, Jenny. You're a much more complex individual than you were at twenty. You bring a lot more to a relationship today than you did then. It's only logical that you should get more out of it."

"I guess." Jenny nodded, comforted by his words. Nick was right. She was a different person.

"We're done, Nick," Jed shouted, "but there's no door on the tent to knock on."

"We're coming." Nick dropped a quick kiss on her nose. "You get them started mixing the plaster of Paris while I get the snakebite kit."

"I wish you wouldn't keep saying that, and what do we need plaster of Paris for?"

"To make casts of animal prints."

"That has possibilities for a child's quilt." Her professional interest was momentarily piqued. Stepping out of the tent, she squinted slightly at the strong sunlight, her eyes taking a moment to adjust to the brilliance after the murky light that had filtered through the green walls of their tent. "It sure is bright."

"Not as bright as it was." Bryan peered up into the sky. "It's supposed to rain later."

"Don't worry," Jenny said. "A little rain never hurt anyone, and besides, the shelters will keep us dry. But we'd better hurry if we want to get your animal-track casts."

The boys scattered to get everything ready, and Jenny watched with an amused smile on her face.

"What's so funny?" Nick emerged from the tent and tied the flap behind him.

"Just how earnest they are."

"Life is earnest when you're nine." Nick chuckled. "Here, you carry the backpack with the lunches and the—"

"Don't say it." Jenny turned and took the sack, suddenly noticing the piece of equipment strapped to his waist.

"That looks like a phone."

"It is. The mobile variety. In case one of the boys breaks something, we can phone for help."

"Good Lord, don't even joke about it," Jenny ordered. "This weekend is going to be accident-free, if I have to clobber all five of them to keep it that way."

9

"GOSH, YOU'RE LUCKY, Jed." Bryan's eyes lingered on Nick.

"Yeah, a black bear track." Jed glanced in satisfaction at the cast in his hand.

"Not that, you clot! I mean that your mother married a neat guy like Nick."

"He's not so neat," Jed scoffed.

"Is so. He knows all about tracking and he was an Eagle Scout and he's taking us camping. My dad said he wouldn't go with us if St. Peter hisself guaranteed him a spot in heaven. And Nick's got a brand-new Corvette," Bryan delivered the coup de grace.

"Yeah," Jed said longingly.

"It's too bad he didn't bring it. Then we coulda sat in it."

"Jenny doesn't like it," Jed admitted.

"Moms never like the really neat stuff." Bryan shrugged. "What was that?" He peered up into the now cloudy sky.

"Rain." Jed helped Bryan lever his cast out of the ground. "You'd better stick it under your shirt, or the water'll ruin it."

"Nick, it's starting to sprinkle," Bryan yelled across the clearing at him.

Nick glanced up through the canopy of reddish-yellow maple leaves that protected him and nodded. "We'd better get back. We need to get supper cooked before the rain gets serious." Turning to Jenny, he asked, "How are you doing, woman?" Then he began to help her repack the casting equipment.

"Wishing I'd brought my book on abnormal psychiatry." Jenny grinned. "Then perhaps I could understand the lure of all this." She waved a dirty, plaster-stained hand around.

"You have no appreciation of nature. How can you look at all this and remain unmoved?"

"It would look just as pretty through a car window and be a lot cleaner, too."

"Bah, you'd never make a pioneer."

"True. I'm strictly an indoor person. Gardening is as close to nature as I'm willing to get." She fell into step beside him as they started back to the campsite.

"Here, let me carry that." Nick took her backpack.

"That's okay, you've already got one. Besides, what about your little speech about all the Scouts carrying their own weight."

"In the first place, you weight's down a little after your bout with the flu. And in the second, as you keep pointing out—"

"I'm not a Scout." She chuckled. "Nick, are we really going to try cooking over an open fire in the rain?"

"This is just a sprinkle. It won't bother anything." Nick reached out and ran a forefinger down her cheek. "Do you want me to take your mind off the weather?"

And he could, too, she admitted as a cascade of shivers shimmered through her at his casual touch. She frowned as she caught sight of his fingers.

"How come you aren't dirty?" She looked down at her own dirt-encrusted nails.

"Because I delegated the dirty work to the ranks." He grinned at her. "You, madame, are rank."

"I'll say," she muttered. "I know I'm going to be sorry I asked, but what are the bathing facilities?"

"We brought a plastic basin, and you can get water from the spigot about a hundred yards from the campsite."

"Hot water?" she asked without much hope of an affirmative answer.

She was right. "It will be if you heat it on the fire."

"Lovely," she muttered. "Eau de woodsmoke-flavored bathwater."

"Did you know that among certain primitive tribes, eau de woodsmoke is considered an aphrodisiac?" He gave her a sideways glance, his eyes brimming with mischief.

"No, I didn't know that." She tried to ignore the shaft of excitement curling through her. "I'll bet you know aphrodisiacs they never even wrote about."

"Of course they didn't write about them. They wouldn't want to share information like that with just anyone. Not only that, but I'm one of the few humans who know the full rites."

"Let me guess. You're willing to fill in the gaps in my education?"

"That wasn't quite what I'd intended to fill."

"Nicholas Sylvester Carlton!"

"What's the matter, Jenny?" Jed looked back at them. "You look kind of funny. All red."

"I . . ." she sputtered.

"Jenny's just upset because I've been explaining to her that areas of her knowledge need filling in," Nick said.

"Well, I suppose anyone could mistake possum tracks for deer tracks," Jed said, trying to console her.

"Nick'll show you," Gordon piped up. "Nick knows all about it."

"If Nick knows what's good for him, he'll stick to his tracks and stay away from Indian lore." She gave him a repressive look. It was bad enough being teased, but in front of the boys there was little she could do to retaliate.

"What Indian lore?" Jed demanded.

"About the Indians who used to live in the Finger Lakes." Nick moved forward among the boys and began the story of Hiawatha's formation of the Iroquois League in the sixteenth century.

Jenny lagged behind, watching Tom's animated face as he drank in Nick's words. Nick had a way with the boys. They responded to his no-nonsense manner. Even Jed, for all his anger over Nick's sudden intrusion into their lives, seemed proud of his friends' acceptance of Nick.

Once they reached the campsite, Nick quickly assigned tasks, and Jenny found herself standing downwind of a smoky fire. She coughed and moved slightly, watching as Tom tried to shield the sputtering flame with his body.

"Don't stand too close to the fire," she ordered.

"Mothers," Tom muttered grumpily, but to Jenny's relief he moved back slightly.

She squinted up into the light rain and then hugged her arms around herself. Unless she missed her guess, the temperature was falling along with the rain. She watched the boys struggle with the fire a bit longer and then said, "Nick brought a mobile phone. We could call for a couple of pizzas, and I could pick them up at the road."

"We're working on a merit badge in cooking," Steve said reprovingly.

"Oh—" Jenny sighed "—I should have known. Sorry I mentioned it."

"S'okay." Jed forgave her. "Women don't understand these things. Do they, Nick?"

"No, but we love them, anyway." Nick gave her a commiserating smile that Jenny barely noticed. Her mind was too full of his words. What would it be like to be loved by Nick? she wondered. To be the focus of his life. It wouldn't be an easy role. Nick was a strong man, both physically and mentally. The woman he loved wouldn't be shielded from all of life's problems. She'd be expected to face life on her own two feet. She'd be his partner, not his dependent.

"Since the boys are doing the cooking, why don't you wash while it's still light enough to see what you're doing?" Nick suggested.

"She can't heat water on my fire," Tom protested. "I need it to cook."

"I wouldn't dream of it," Jenny assured him. "I'm a big devotee of cold showers."

"I think I'm going to be the one taking cold showers this weekend," Nick whispered with an explicit look at her breasts as she passed him on her way to the tent.

Jenny glanced down, and a flush tinted her cheeks as she realized that the light rain had dampened her sweater to the point that her curves were faithfully outlined. Hastily she yanked the wet wool away from her and promptly sneezed.

"Are you catching a cold?" Nick demanded.

"Of course she isn't," Jed scoffed. "You can't get a cold from a wetting."

"Can't get any sympathy, either." She hurried into the tent to find the plastic basin.

"Don't be too long. Dinner will be ready soon," Tom called after her.

It might be ready, but would it be edible? she wondered. To her dismay it wasn't, but she munched her way through the half-raw potato and burned hamburger with a stoicism born of love.

After dinner the boys gathered in the tent and carefully went over their plaster casts, discussing the animals that had made the tracks while Jenny sat on the ice chest and tallied her receipts for the week. She was trying to decide how much extra Christmas material to risk ordering when the boys' moans brought her back to the present.

"But, Nick, it's only nine-thirty," Jed wailed.

"It'll be ten by the time you've all gotten ready for bed. Now hop to it." Nick ignored their grumbles.

"May I help?" She stuffed her bookkeeping records in her knapsack.

"The whole idea of camping is to teach self-reliance." Nick walked over to her and held up the camp lantern, studying her face. "Besides, you're looking rather pale." He ran a gentle fingertip across the dark smudges under her eyes, and Jenny felt her heartbeat accelerate. "I know the doctor said you were completely recovered from the flu, but—"

"I am." Jenny moved off the ice chest, hoping her action appeared casual. She couldn't bear him to realize how sensitized she was becoming to his casual touch. An admission of that magnitude would raise too many questions. And they weren't questions she wanted to explore, not even in her own mind.

"Then why are you pale?" Nick frowned at her.

"All this fresh air poisoned me." Jenny dug out her serviceable flannel nightgown.

"Jenny, I'm serious!"

"You think I'm not." She gave him a wry look. "You and the boys might think camping's a great experience, but as far as I'm concerned, it's strictly for the birds."

"And the raccoons and the deer and the foxes." Nick waved toward the plaster casts neatly piled on one side of their tent. "You just haven't gotten used to it."

"One doesn't get used to camping. One endures it."

"Nick." Jed called from outside the tent flap. "We want to go to the bathroom."

"You know where it is."

"But, Nick," Gordon piped up, "it's clear down the path and it's dark."

"Real dark," Steve threw in.

"And we've only got one light," Tom added.

"And if we each take it into the rest room with us, then the ones outside won't be able to see," Jed finished up.

"All right, I'll be along in a moment. Start up the path." Nick picked up the lantern.

"Hey, just a minute there." Jenny's voice stopped him. "If you take the lantern, I'll be left in the dark."

"Which is exactly where you want to be," Nick said. "Leaving the light on in the tent while you're changing will outline your figure against the walls. Graphically."

"Oh! Well, in that case, you go with our intrepid explorers, and I'll get ready for bed."

"Quickly," Nick ordered. "The rain's bringing the temperature down fast. I'll be back in a few minutes." He left, plunging the tent into darkness.

Hurriedly she slipped into her nightgown, then cautiously crept into her sleeping bag. A series of shudders shook her as the cold material attacked her warm feet, quickly reducing them to blocks of ice.

"Oh, for a pair of wool socks." She shivered, waiting for her body warmth to heat the icy material. For some reason it didn't. She kept getting colder and colder until the chill seemed to permeate her very bones. She huddled in a protective ball, clenched her chattering teeth and prepared to endure. If a bunch of nine-year-olds could stand it, so could she.

"It's me, Jenny." Nick strode back into the tent.

"Gr-r-great," she chattered.

"What's wrong with you?"

"I'm cold, of course, but don't worry. I'll either warm up, or else I'll freeze right through. Either way, I won't feel a thing."

Nick walked over to her and held his lantern over her huddled body. "You shouldn't be— Your sleeping bag's touching the tent walls!"

"S-s-so? The canvas looks sturdy enough to me."

"It's only waterproof as long as nothing's touching it. Where your sleeping bag's touching, the walls are leaking. Your bag is acting like a wick, drawing the rain into it. The reason you can't get warm is because your bedding is damp."

"That's the dumbest thing I've ever heard of." Jenny was outraged.

"You can say that again," he said in exasperation. "Out!" He yanked her zipper open and hauled her out of the sleeping bag.

Jenny stumbled as her icy feet refused to support her.

"You're more trouble than that whole pack of nine-year-olds." He sighed. "Hold still a minute while I feel your nightgown."

"Oh, lovely." Jenny giggled. "That's all this evening needs to cap it off. An irate camper with a nightgown fetish."

"Wet," he said in disgust. "Take it off."

"The eternal masculine refrain." Jenny's giggles escalated into laughter.

"Dammit, woman." Nick pressed the back of his hand against her icy cheek. "You're cold."

"Jed assures me— What are you doing?" she squeaked as he grabbed the hem of her nightgown.

"Getting this off you. Hold still." He ruthlessly pulled the gown over her head.

Jenny shivered and then sneezed as the cold air in the tent engulfed her. "I didn't bring another nightgown," she wailed.

"Don't worry, I did." He moved through the blackness with surefooted precision.

"You did? I wouldn't have thought you were the night-gown type."

"What I am is the prepared type. Here." He shoved something soft into her hands.

"What is it?" Jenny squinted down at it.

"A spare T-shirt. Put it on."

"You wouldn't happen to have a spare sleeping bag, would you?" Her voice was muffled as she slipped into it.

"No, we'll share mine. Get in."

"Share yours?" she repeated blankly.

"We are married, woman. Now get in."

Climbing into his bag, she wiggled into a comfortable position. His sleeping bag was bigger than the one she'd borrowed from Bryan's mother, but it still wasn't meant for two. She rolled over on her side and cautiously stretched her feet toward the end.

A subtle blend of aromas drifted up from the material to color her perceptions. Cautiously she sniffed, trying to catalog them. There was a faint lingering trace of a man's cologne, along with a subtle spicy fragrance. She sniffed again. Sandalwood, she recognized it. Was everything in the Middle East sprinkled with sandalwood? she wondered, her curiosity dissolving as Nick slipped in beside her and zipped the bag shut. Jenny found herself squashed between the side of the bag and Nick's chest. Her arms were pinned between them, and her cold legs were entangled with his. He shifted slightly, and his hair-covered thighs scraped over her much softer ones.

Jenny suppressed a groan as each and every spot where they were touching burst into clamoring life. She wiggled her arms again. "Um, Nick, I hate to mention this, but—"

"Then don't."

"But I have to. The thing is . . . I think I may be just the tiniest bit claustrophobic," she confided. "I get nervous when I can't move my arms."

"Think about something else."

"What else is there to think about in this benighted place?" she wailed.

"There's always me." He slipped an arm around her and pulled her even closer.

"Hmm." Her voice came out in a shaky sigh as she felt her breasts swell with pleasure at being crushed against his hard chest. Her face was tucked into his neck, and his emerging beard stabbed the soft skin of her forehead.

Grasping her waist, he levered her upward.

Jenny gasped as her body rubbed over his. She tried to tug down the T-shirt, which had ridden up to her waist, but they were pressed too close together. She could feel his growing passion, and her own desire tightened around her like a noose.

His hand slipped beneath her shirt to cup her small breast. Slowly he rotated his palm over the hardening tip.

"Ah, Nick." She arched into his hand. "I want—"

"Nick?" Tom's voice came from outside. "Nick? I gotta go to the bathroom, and they won't go with me."

Nick's caressing hand froze. "You just *went* to the bathroom," he said.

"But I gotta go again. I gotta!" Tom sounded close to tears.

"For heaven's sake, tell him to go in the bushes." Jenny groaned.

"After having given them a fifteen-minute lecture on the ecology and the importance of not upsetting it?" Nick sighed. "I'm afraid, in this case, we're hoisted on our own petard." Raising his voice, he called, "Just a minute, Tom, while I get dressed." He unzipped the bag, flung back the covers and leaped to his feet. Jenny listened as he yanked on his jeans, her eyes straining to see his superb physique.

"Keep the sleeping bag warm," Nick flung over his shoulder. "I'll be right back."

She could keep the whole tent warm simply from the strength of the passion Nick had aroused, Jenny thought ruefully. Her whole body tingled as if she'd touched a live wire. She took a deep breath and focused on the tent pole, trying hard to steady her breathing. She didn't want to appear any more unsophisticated than she already had.

By the time Nick returned, Jenny was able to greet him with a fair degree of composure. A composure that immediately developed cracks when his leg brushed against hers as he slipped into the bag.

He put an arm around her body and pulled her up against him with a casualness she envied. As if they'd been married for years. Or as if their physical contact didn't mean all that much to him. The unwelcome thought surfaced only to sink again beneath her reawakening excitement.

"Sorry to be so long," Nick whispered against her temple, "but I had to search the whole damn john for spiders while the kid stood outside jumping up and down on one leg."

"That sounds like Tom." Jenny chuckled. "He's got this thing about spiders."

"And I've got this thing about you." His chilled lips wandered across her eyebrow and down over her small straight nose. His arm tightened, pulling her even closer to his chest. The wiry hair brushed abrasively over the soft peaks of her breasts, hardening them into buds of desire.

"Your skin feels like satin, Jenny, cool, silky satin." His fingertips played over her cheekbones, tracing her jawline down to her small determined chin. "It makes a man want to kiss it." His lips brushed gently over hers. Tremors of reaction slipped over her skin, and a small moan escaped her as his lips moved down to explore her throat. When he reached the hollow at the base of her neck, his tongue flicked out, stroking lightly over the skin.

Her fingers dug into his shoulders. A heaviness was growing deep in her abdomen. A heaviness that increased with every stroke of his caressing tongue.

She flattened her hands on his broad chest and rubbed her palms over the small tight masculine nipples buried deep in the dark cloud. His reaction was instantaneous. He rolled onto her, trapping her hands between them. His leg pushed between her thighs, and his mouth closed over her lips.

Jenny's mouth opened welcomingly at the aggressive thrust of his tongue. His warm, coffee-flavored breath filled first her mouth and then her mind as his kiss deepened. She arched her lower body into the heavy weight of his thighs, and the throbbing in her abdomen tightened to the breaking point.

"Nick?" Steve's voice was an unbearable intrusion, and Jenny instinctively pressed closer to Nick in negation of it.

"Nick, our shelter's leaking," Gordon called out.

"Damn, damn, damn!" Nick's muffled curse was a litany as he jumped out of bed and yanked on his jeans.

"I'm coming," he yelled at the boys. "I'm sorry, Jenny."

"Me, too," she said ruefully. "I'm beginning to think that some things simply weren't meant to be."

"This was." He dropped a hard kiss on her lips. "I'll be right back."

His estimation was slightly off. It was almost fifteen minutes before he stalked back into the tent, muttering to himself.

"Did you fix it?" Jenny asked.

"What I'd like to fix is them." Nick tore off his clothes with flattering haste. "But the roof really was leaking, so we shoved the cots together in the second shelter and put Steve in with Jed, Bryan and Tom."

"How nice," she muttered with complete uninterest. The only thing that did interest her was the feel of his body slipping back into the sleeping bag.

"You're cold." She used her observation as an excuse to run her hands down over his chest. She could feel his hard ribs beneath the supple texture of his skin, and she traced one around his chest. "Poor man," she breathed, "you're missing ribs."

"You want to count ribs?" He suddenly pushed her onto her back and crouched on the cot beside her.

Jenny peered up at him through slitted eyes. He looked enormous, looming above her, but she felt no fear, only a rising sense of excitement.

Nick pushed the edge of her T-shirt up and placed his warm lips at the bottom of her rib cage. Jenny jerked convulsively at the heated touch of his mouth. She clutched his head, and her fingers sank into his thick, rain-dampened hair.

His hands closed over hers, and he gently pulled them back down to the cot. "You're disturbing my concentration," he whispered.

"Believe me, it's mutual." She gasped as his lips slowly began to trail upward. Wave after wave of desire crashed through her, and she wiggled frantically beneath his searching lips.

He paused when he reached the soft base of her breast. "How can I count your ribs with this protrusion in the way? I'll have to detour." He began to trace around it with the tip of his tongue. A pervasive heat spread from his touch, and Jenny twisted restively.

"Nick, please," she pleaded.

"But what do you want? This, perhaps?" His mouth closed over the puckered tip of her breast, and he drew it into the hot cavern. Slowly, methodically, he scraped his tongue over the sensitized peak, rubbing back and forth as Jenny arched into him. His hand moved down over her quivering stomach, and he lightly scored his nails over her soft flesh.

Her skin felt hot, burning under the impact of what he was doing. She cupped his face, agitatedly running her fingertips over his roughened cheeks. She suddenly froze as she felt his hand slip lower to press over the apex of her thighs.

"Don't be shy, my sweet," Nick whispered. "Let yourself enjoy it." His finger probed her soft, moist core.

Jenny gasped as a white-hot explosion pulsed through her. Slowly he rubbed, and the coil of tension within her wound tighter. She opened for him, lifting herself against his caress as muffled whimpers of delight escaped through her clenched teeth.

"Yes, that's it." Nick's voice was husky as he moved over her. She strained into him as she felt his blunt warmth beckoning, luring her toward untold delights.

"Nick!" The plaintive wail from right outside the door had the effect of a douse of cold water.

"No," she protested, "not now."

"What!" Nick roared.

"I heard something behind the shelter," Gordon moaned, "and I'm afraid to stay there by myself. I want to go into the other shelter, even if my side is dry."

"I know where I'd like to send you," Nick muttered. "Gordon, go back to the shelter and—"

"No!" Gordon's frightened voice sounded closer. "I can hear something in the bushes."

"All right, I'm coming! How the hell do parents ever have more than one kid?" he bit out.

"I don't believe this." Jenny began to laugh uproariously. Here she was, in the middle of the most incredibly exciting experience of her life, and they were constantly being interrupted. "There's no justice in this world," she said, gasping.

"No satisfaction, either," Nick said sourly as he slipped into his jeans. "I'm going to move Gordon's cot and stay with them till they fall asleep. Maybe then we can have some privacy."

"I wouldn't count on it." Jenny went off into another gale of laughter.

"Damn!" Nick glanced longingly at the dim outline of her body. "Maybe . . ."

"Nick, I'm getting wet," Gordon wailed.

"No, I guess not." He heaved a sigh. "You know, Jenny, you're missing out on a fortune. You ought to rent that quintet out to Planned Parenthood. Any couple contemplating having a baby could spend a weekend with them. I guarantee you the population would plummet."

"Aw, the boys aren't that bad," Jenny protested. "Besides, babies are kind of cute."

Jenny's would be. The thought popped full-blown into Nick's mind. Small and soft, with little tufts of bright red hair. Yes, Jenny's babies would undoubtedly be cute. His eyes narrowed as he pictured how she'd look pregnant—her belly swollen with his child, her breasts heavy, her face glowing with anticipation.

"Nick!" Gordon yelped.

A baby that would undoubtedly grow into a facsimile of that, he thought ruefully as he turned to leave.

10

"HOW WAS the camping trip?" Sarah Pearson handed Jenny a bolt of cloth.

Jenny shuddered with remembered horror. "I don't think I'll ever be able to look at the great outdoors again without a queasy feeling in the pit of my stomach."

"Give me two and a half yards of that. Bryan had fun. He said, and I quote, 'It was splendiferous.'"

Parts of it had certainly been. A soft, dreamy smile curved her lips as she remembered their sharing of the sleeping bag, and how, when the boys had at last fallen asleep, their lovemaking had exploded into a conflagration that had left them both shaken at the violence of their reaction.

"You did have a bad weekend." Sarah sympathized. "You're still half-asleep."

"Sorry." Jenny began to measure the bright red material. "Two and a half yards, you said?"

"Um-hm, and a yard of that batting on the roll. I'm piecing a quilt for the doll I'm dressing for the church's Christmas baskets this year. I'm going to make it some clothes, too, but I want to use permanent press for them. I wish you carried other materials besides just cotton. As a matter of fact, that brings me to something I've been meaning to talk to you about ever since you got married."

"Oh?"

"It's obvious that once Nick repairs the farmhouse, you'll be moving out there. I mean, a farmer really has to live on the place, and besides, that big old house is perfect for a family."

"I guess." Jenny gave the only reply possible. She could hardly tell Sarah that her conclusion was based on a false premise: that she and Nick intended to remain married.

"Which will leave your flat empty," Sarah continued, "and I was thinking that you could sell nonquilting types of materials up there. I've already done some research and I've found several outlets where we could buy Health-Tex, Carter and Burlington Mills surplus fabrics. At really great prices, Jenny."

"We?" Jenny latched on to the word.

"I'd like to manage it for you on a commission basis. Now that Billy's in first grade, I don't have to be home all day and I want to start earning a little to put aside for the boys' education. College is so expensive."

"True," Jenny agreed.

"And you have such a tremendous trade that if only a fraction of your regular customers bought, we'd still make a good profit." She paused and eyed Jenny hopefully. "Since I'd be on commission, you wouldn't have to pay me a salary. Your only outlay would be for remodeling the flat and for buying the material."

"You've certainly got it all worked out," Jenny said slowly.

Sarah picked up her package. "I'm not trying to rush you into a commitment. Just give it some thought."

"All right, but I doubt I'll be making a decision soon," Jenny stalled. "Nick and I haven't even discussed moving out to the farm."

"You've only been married a couple of weeks. But pretty soon you'll start to surface from the euphoria of being newlyweds. As a matter of fact, that camping trip was probably your first step toward a more normal life."

"That camping trip qualifies as a violation of the Geneva convention," Jenny said glumly. "When I die, I'll probably find out that hell is a giant campground."

Sarah laughed. "You never were the active type. Remember how in gym you were always pretending you'd sprained your ankle?"

"I was very inventive." Jenny chuckled.

"Well, you'd better polish up your excuses because you're going to need them, what with Nick taking over as Scoutmaster."

"Don't I know it." Jenny grimaced. "But maybe they'll find someone else to lead the troop. After all, Nick only agreed to do it on a temporary basis."

"Dream on. No one's going to volunteer. Nick'll be stuck until Jed's out of Scouting. And by that time you could have a couple novice Scouts yourself. Now don't forget to think about my idea."

"I won't." Jenny watched Sarah leave, her mind occupied with images of Nick's children. They'd be sturdy little facsimiles of him with bright blue eyes, dark brown hair and his square, determined jaw. And probably always into trouble. She pulled her imagination up short. Nick had been very specific about not wanting any children. Illogically she found the thought depressing.

JENNY HURRIEDLY DRIED her hands on the kitchen towel and reached for the phone. "Hello?"

"Is Nick there?"

"I'm sorry, Adelaide." Jenny had no trouble placing the voice. "Nick's at a fruit growers' meeting tonight. May I have him call you back later?"

"No, that's okay. I didn't want anything specific. I just..."

"Well, if you didn't want anything specific, would I do instead?" Jenny couldn't bring herself to hang up. Adelaide sounded so despondent.

"You must be wishing I was at the other end of the earth." Adelaide sighed. "I wish I were, too. With Don..." Her voice broke on a sob.

"You'll be with Don soon." Jenny injected all the confidence she could into her voice. "Both Murad and Nick say so. And while they might not want to upset you, they'd have no reason to lie to me."

"That's true," Adelaide said slowly. "They wouldn't. Oh, Jenny, I wish he'd never gone back, but he was so determined to finish his contract so we could get the bonus and buy that inn in Oregon."

"Innkeeping sounds like quite a career change," Jenny murmured encouragingly, knowing that Adelaide simply wanted to talk about her husband.

"Oh, his father ran a ski lodge in Vermont," Adelaide began.

Jenny leaned back and prepared to listen, thinking it was the least she could do for the poor woman. But what would be the most? The unwelcome thought intruded. What would Nick feel bound to do for Adelaide if Murad was wrong and Don Witton didn't make it home? *Don't borrow trouble*, she told herself, forcing herself to concentrate on Adelaide's rambling monologue.

NICK ROUNDED the side of the shop and paused as he caught sight of Jenny through the front window. She was rearranging a rack of fabric. He watched in fascination as she reached up to the top shelf and the silky material of her blouse stretched tautly over her small breasts. He clenched his fingers as he remembered the soft weight of them filling his palm, the dark rose nipples hardening beneath his caresses.

His eyes slipped down over her straight back to linger on the gently rounded curves of her narrow hips. He could feel his body hardening with passion as in his mind he removed her jeans. She'd be wearing a minuscule pair of lacy panties, he decided. For such a utilitarian dresser she wore surprisingly sexy underwear.

But then Jenny was full of surprises. Not the least of which was the vibrantly passionate woman who lurked beneath the surface of her calm, competent exterior. A passionate woman who had irreversibly changed the memories he'd always held of little Jenny Ryton. Only now she was Jenny Carlton. A surge of satisfaction welled within him. Jenny belonged to him. All that passion and warmth was reserved for him. But for how long? He frowned as he remembered that Jenny had been quite explicit about wanting their marriage to last only one year. But that was before she'd come to know him. How did she feel about him now? he wondered. Was there a chance that she saw him fitting into her life on a permanent basis? He rubbed the bridge of his nose thoughtfully. It was hard to tell. Jenny was such a reserved person. She certainly didn't need him for financial support. A wry grin lifted his lips as he remembered the seventy-five thousand she'd given him. No, Jenny was more than capable of supporting herself. If she needed him at all, it was emotionally, he thought, remembering her explosive reaction to his lovemaking. But did she consider that a plus or a minus in their relationship? He also remembered her confused uncertainty and her absurd sense of guilt.

He grimaced. Jenny had gotten into the habit of channeling all her emotions into the maternal role, and she was very leery of venturing into wider and potentially more rewarding fields. It was up to him to convince her that it was worth the risk.

Squaring his shoulders, he walked into the shop.

"Be with you in a moment," Jenny threw over her shoulder as the bell above the door tinkled. She stood on tiptoe and tried to shove the bolt of dark blue print on the top rack.

"Need help?" Nick's deep voice from right behind her caused her to jump, and the bolt slipped. He reached around her and rescued the material.

The heat from his large body warmed her back and his muscular forearm brushed against her as he put it on the top shelf. A shiver chased across her skin, and a dark coil of excitement exploded in her chest. Closing her eyes, she slowly exhaled and tried not to let her instantaneous response to him become obvious. She had more pride than that.

"You need a step stool." To her relief he moved back and she was able to regain her equilibrium.

"I know. When I ordered these new racks, I got them eight feet high instead of the usual six, and the top shelf's a shade too tall."

"Or you're a shade too short." Nick's eyes twinkled.

"I'm not too short," she insisted.

"Not for some things." A slow smile curved his lips. "As a matter of fact, lying beside me, you're exactly—"

"Nick! Not here." She shot a warning glance toward the storeroom door.

"Oh, I had no intention of doing it here," he said in mock innocence. "I was thinking—"

"You weren't thinking," she said primly.

"True enough. I was feeling." He glanced down at his hardening body. "You seem to have a very fundamental effect on me."

"Poor you."

"No, I'm beginning to realize just how unpoor you make me. Now then," he said briskly, "you haven't had your lunch yet, have you?"

"No," she said slowly, much more interested in his comment than his question. Unpoor. Just what did he mean? Was it a reference to the seventy-five thousand she'd given him?

"You ought to keep a few cookies behind the cash register." Nick's rueful tones broke into her thoughts.

"Cookies?" She blinked. "What for?"

"To raise your blood sugar level." He eyed her critically. "So you don't keep going off into trances."

"I was thinking," she excused herself.

"Forget thinking and come out to the farm with me. Marge can mind the shop."

"Why?"

"Because it's a glorious October day, and I thought I'd go see if any of those apple trees survived. You can show me where they were planted. We shouldn't be more than an hour."

Jenny savored the strength of the pleasure that surged through her at the thought of spending even an hour with Nick. Just the two of them. Alone. It was a pleasure that seemed to grow with every added exposure to him. It fed on itself. Growing and infiltrating her whole personality.

"Just let me tell Marge where I'm going."

"I'll meet you out front. Don't dawdle."

Don't dawdle, indeed! Jenny's eyes sparkled with annoyance as she stuck her head in the back room. "Marge, I'm going out to the farm with Nick. I'll be back in about an hour."

"Take your time." Marge glanced up from the box of thimbles she was unpacking. "I can cope with the shop."

Probably better than I can cope with Nick, Jenny thought, but the knowledge did nothing to diminish her sense of anticipation as she hurried out to the parking lot. Nick was right. She sniffed the crisp air. It was a glorious day. At the moment. She cast a weather eye at the sky. There were dark clouds to the northeast.

"The sub and Coke are for you." Nick handed a sack to her. "You can eat on the way out."

"Thanks." A warm feeling engulfed her at his thoughtfulness. Every once in a while it was nice to have someone take care of her needs, she admitted. Even if it was only a little thing like making sure she got her lunch. With a feeling of contentment she opened the sandwich wrapper and began to eat as they sped toward the farm.

Nick parked in front of the barn and asked, "Where are the apple trees?"

"That way." She gestured with the Coke cup. "Beyond the pasture behind the barn."

"Hmm." Nick peered thoughtfully in the direction she was pointing. "Now that you mention it, I vaguely remember my father saying that it would be good land for an orchard. Come on." He took her arm, and Jenny hurried along beside him, her whole concentration on the feel of his hard fingers curled around her wrist.

"About what I expected." Nick frowned at knee-high weeds, which choked the huge orchard. Hundreds of trees were loaded with red and yellow apples. But many trees were lifeless, their bare branches giving stark evidence of their neglect.

Jenny picked what looked like a Golden Russet apple and looked closely at it. It was full of wormholes. Regretfully she dropped it into the tall grass.

She watched Nick as he walked through the orchard, pausing occasionally to check a particular tree. It would take an incredible amount of work to get this orchard producing salable fruit, she realized. Even the trees that had survived looked as if they'd never been pruned.

Perhaps this neglected orchard was a heaven-sent opportunity. Nick seemed unwilling to plant anything or to buy anything new, but the trees were already here. Moreover, his father had planted them. Maybe she could subtly appeal to the love Nick had for his father to convince him to get the orchard into shape. It would certainly keep him busy and, hopefully, would help to allay the guilt he felt over what was happening to Don Witton. Especially if Murad should prove to be wrong and the negotiations dragged out over the winter.

She hurried after Nick, catching up with him at the far end of the orchard. He was fingering the withered remains of a fruit that still clung to a tree.

"These aren't all apples," he said. "This looks like a peach or a nectarine."

"What you need is a fruit expert to tell you what you've got."

"I already know what I've got. A mess." He wiped his fingers on his denim-clad thighs, and Jenny's eyes followed the movement, her eyes straying to his masculine shape.

"This whole orchard should be cut for firewood." He glanced disparagingly around.

"Some of it, but it looks to me as if at least half, maybe two-thirds, could be salvaged."

"Why bother?"

"Why not?" Jenny tried to keep her voice casual. "Your father went to a lot of trouble to plant it. To say nothing of expense. Dwarf fruit trees don't come cheap, even in quantity. A field this size of producing fruit trees would add quite a lot of value to the farm."

"Maybe, but as you pointed out, what's needed is an expert opinion."

"The Geneva Experiment Station's only an hour away. They have hundreds of agricultural experts, and I'm sure they'd be glad to help."

Maybe he could reclaim it, Nick considered. It would be satisfying to turn this derelict orchard into a producing one. And with Murad about to gain Witton's freedom, he'd have plenty of time.

"I'll call the experiment station tomorrow morning," Nick said, and Jenny glanced down at her feet to hide the triumph that lit her eyes. She'd done it. She'd succeeded in adding one more tendril to the flimsy ties that bound him to Litton.

"Tomorrow, I'll..." Nick paused as a raindrop splattered on his hand. "Good." He looked up into the darkening sky with satisfaction. "It's going to rain."

Jenny followed his glance. "It's going to pour." She began to hurry toward the car. "And why's that good? You like getting wet?"

"It might have its compensations." His bright blue eyes focused on her breasts, and Jenny felt her breathing develop a staccato rhythm. "I can see it now. The rain soaking that thin blouse you're wearing, making it stick to your breasts, their nipples jutting, chilled and hard, against the fabric. Have I ever told you you have beautifully shaped breasts, Jenny?"

"Umm, no," she muttered, wondering how she was going to be able to carry off this conversation without sounding as if she was terminally shy. She watched his gaze slip lower to land on the soft swell of her abdomen. Fearing that his comments were about to get even more intimate, she scrambled to sidetrack him.

"Why do you want it to rain?"

"Because I want to check the roof. Come on." He grabbed her arm as the skies opened and began to pour, and pulled her through the open barn door.

Jenny blinked in the dim light. "That's right. You fixed the roof, didn't you?"

"Uh-huh." Picking up a flashlight, he headed toward the steps that led to the loft. "And now I want to see if there're any leaks."

"I'll help." Jenny followed him up.

11

"LORD, IT'S SPOOKY up here." Jenny paused at the top of the stairs and peered into the gloom of the cavernous loft.

"You rang?"

Jenny found herself pinned in the powerful beam of the flashlight Nick was holding. "Talk about delusions of grandeur," she scoffed.

"You don't think I'd make a good deity?" Nick chuckled.

"A deity, perhaps. *The* deity, not by a long shot. You're much too..." Jenny focused on his shoulders, their breadth emphasized by the rain-dampened T-shirt that clung to him. Slowly her eyes wandered lower, down his flat abdomen, his powerful thighs and the long length of his legs. He did look rather like a warrior god of long ago. Powerful, elemental and untamed. A savage crack of lightning added to the illusion, and Jenny shivered as desire shafted through her.

"Too what?"

"Too earthy," she finally said. "You haven't a broad enough outlook."

"Nonsense, I never look beyond a broad."

"Nick Carlton, don't be vulgar."

"It's not vulgar to look." He walked slowly toward her, his feet making rustling sounds in the heavy coating of hay that covered the floor. "Not just to look." His voice became husky as he slowly played the beam over her slim body.

Jenny could feel her mouth drying as the warming touch of the light moved back and forth across the swelling curves of her breasts. Their nipples hardened, pushing against the thin material of her blouse in mute appeal.

"No, looking's not vulgar. As a matter of fact, with a sexy little piece like you it's a foregone conclusion." Nick came to a halt a scant six inches from her, and it took all of Jenny's willpower not to retreat in the face of his blatant masculinity.

There was something about him that made her feel threatened. Made her feel that she should take to her heels and run. And yet, logically, she knew that her reaction made no sense. Nick would never hurt her. She'd stake her life on it. So why did she feel endangered? She worried the question around in her mind.

"As a matter of fact, I'm not so sure that touching's vulgar, either. At least, not all touching." He tossed the flashlight onto a pile of hay bales. "For example, shaking hands is touching, and that's not vulgar, is it?"

Jenny peered up at him, barely hearing his words. She could feel the warmth of his heavily muscled body pouring off him in waves. Engulfing her, tugging her toward him. The musky scent of his skin mixed with the faint fragrance of summer sunshine and dried flowers that was coming from the hay. It was an intoxicating blend of desire and dreamy summer days.

"And then there's the social kiss," Nick continued hypnotically. His lips brushed ever so lightly over her soft cheek. "This can't be vulgar. Even the minister's wife does it. Although in certain circles, social kissing is a little more intimate." He moved closer still. "It's done on the lips." Nick's compulsive voice lured her deeper into the spell he was weaving. A spell she seemed powerless to resist.

He leaned over and rubbed his hard lips across hers, bringing them to tingling life. "Of course," he whispered, "if they're really good friends, they might add a touch like this . . ." The tip of his tongue traced over her quivering bottom lip, and Jenny shuddered. Slowly she exhaled, trying to even the erratic cadence of her breathing.

"Of course, touching includes a lot of gray areas in our culture." He reached out and slowly traced the curves of her breast with hard fingertips.

Jenny sucked in her breath in an audible gasp as waves of longing surged through her.

"I don't . . ."

"You don't think touching like this is vulgar?"

As if in a dream, Jenny felt him remove her blouse and bra.

"You're probably right," he continued in a meditative tone. "I've noticed that our culture seems to allow quite a bit of touching with the hands."

"And I've noticed that I'm half naked," Jenny responded, feeling she should call a halt to his actions but unable to think of one compelling reason to do so that would outweigh the stark desire pulsing through her.

"Now that's what I call observant." Nick sounded approving, and Jenny chuckled. "If we're going to investigate this question properly, it's essential that you pay attention to what we're doing."

Pay attention! The only way she *couldn't* notice what he was doing would be if she were dead.

Nick lowered his head, and Jenny froze as she felt his warm breath waft over her breasts. "Touching with the lips somehow seems so much more intimate, doesn't it?" As if to illustrate his point he began to nuzzle her soft curves. Her skin seemed to burn where he caressed her.

She clutched his head and tried to hold his wandering lips in one spot.

"No, no." Nick's hands closed over her fingers, and he tugged them down to her side where he anchored them.

"You're introducing too many variables. You aren't supposed to be touching me. Now, where was I?" He paused, his mouth a fraction of an inch from the tip of her right breast. "How about if I were to try something else?" he mused. "Say..." His tongue suddenly darted out and stroked abrasively over her dusky-rose nipple.

"Nick!" Her voice escaped on an anguished gasp as the quivering in her abdomen tightened painfully.

"That's definitely more intimate." Nick's voice was husky as he repeated the caress, and Jenny twisted restively in his arms. "I think I've got something here."

A sigh of anticipation escaped her as she felt the hard brush of his fingers on her stomach as he slowly lowered the zipper on her jeans. His mouth inexorably followed, painting an intricate pattern with his tongue.

"I can't stand any more of this." She strained against his confining hands.

"Of course you can. You underestimate yourself."

Jenny took heart from the unsteady sound of his voice. He was as affected by what he was doing as she was. If she could just give him a gentle push and send him beyond the limits of his control... She shook her head, trying to clear her passion-fogged mind. It was hopeless. Her whole being was concentrating on Nick slowly pulling her jeans down over her legs. A whimper escaped her parted lips as he began to plant stinging kisses on the soft skin of her inner thigh.

"You're such a delight to touch, Jenny. So smooth and silky." His voice sounded far away. The only reality for her was the feel of his hot, searching mouth.

"I want..." Her high-pitched voice echoed through the loft.

"Another form of touching?" He suddenly swung her up in his arms and strode toward a deep pile of loose hay.

Placing her on it, he yanked off her jeans, which were clinging to her ankles, then stripped off his own clothes.

Totally oblivious to the tiny pinpricks of the hay stems, Jenny stared longingly at him. The sight of his superb body filled her mind to the exclusion of all else. She wanted him. Needed him desperately to satisfy the longing that consumed her. She held her arms out to him as he dropped down beside her.

His right arm slipped beneath her, turning her into his chest, and his other hand cupped the center of her desire. Slowly his fingers probed, rubbing tantalizingly over the satiny flesh until Jenny thought she'd scream with the agony of wanting him. Frantically she clutched his shoulders and tried to wiggle closer to him.

Finally, to her infinite relief, he responded, moving over her and completing their embrace with one powerful thrust of his body.

Jenny released her breath on an exquisite sigh as, for a second, simply the feel of him within her was sufficient. But only for a second. Her need began to spiral out of control as desire became a compulsion to seek satisfaction. She arched into him, forcing him deeper. She felt that if he stopped now, she'd never be whole again. A feeling Nick obviously shared, for he cupped her slender hips and held her still as with methodical precision he drove them both to a state of mindless ecstasy. Then, their passion spent, they lay still in the hay, arms clasped tightly about one another.

After a while Nick spoke, his voice seeming to come from far away. "I have reached a conclusion."

"Umm." Jenny nuzzled her face into his sweat-dampened chest. Somehow she'd wound up on top of him. She tried to remember how it had happened and gave it up as unimportant. All that mattered was the magnitude of the pleasure they'd just shared. She stretched in supreme contentment and then chuckled as she felt him stirring against her leg.

She'd suspected from the beginning that Nick Carlton was a virile man. What she hadn't suspected was that she was a very passionate woman. A chill feathered over her skin at the implication of the thought. What was going to happen when their marriage ended next year and she found it necessary to cut out a part of her life that was bringing her so much fulfillment? Refusing to let concern over the future destroy her enjoyment of the present, she forced the worry to the back of her mind and concentrated instead on what Nick was saying.

"No touching between us could ever be vulgar," Nick stated.

"That's for sure," Jenny murmured happily.

JENNY WINCED at the sound of the door banging as Jed stalked into the apartment. He flung his book bag on the table and dropped onto the couch.

"You forgot to kick the cat." Jenny tried for a light touch to counter his evident fury. Had Nick upset him again? Or had he upset Nick? She hoped not. They'd been getting along so well since the camping trip. She hated the thought of her peaceful evenings disintegrating into the open warfare of the first week of their marriage.

Jed scowled. "We haven't got a cat."

"I was speaking metaphorically. What happened?"

"I hate her!" The low intensity of Jed's voice was far more alarming than a shout would have been.

"Her?" Jenny latched on to the word. "Not Nick?"

"Nick's okay," he conceded grudgingly. "If he'd just teach me to drive his Corvette. Jenny—" he eyed her calculatingly "—you could ask him to teach me."

"If I thought there was the slightest chance that he'd actually do it, I'd take that overpriced heap of nuts and bolts and drive it into a tree."

"Women!"

Jenny grinned at the echo of Nick's tone in Jed's exclamation. "Now tell me who's she and what did she do?"

"Miss Harmon," Jed hissed. "She gave me an *F* on my math test and then told the entire class I hadn't gotten a single problem right."

"I find that hard to believe."

"She did! She—"

"Not that." Jenny sighed. "That I can believe, but how could you miss all the problems?"

"I didn't. The test was real boring stuff. Adding columns of six-digit numbers. I finished in ten minutes, so I started redoing them in base eight and then base twelve. It was my base twelve sheet she took. I told her that wasn't the test, but she said that since I was working on it during test time, it had to be."

"And, of course, the answers in base twelve are entirely different from base ten."

"She's a bitch!"

"Don't swear, and besides, that's an oversimplification. She's simply a rather dumb woman who feels threatened by anyone who thinks faster than she does. I guess I'll have to go see her again."

"You know, Jenny, when you think about it, I don't know why Litton doesn't have a hit man. We could have used him twice just this past month."

"Violence doesn't solve problems. It merely creates others," she felt obligated to point out.

"I'll take almost any problem instead of Miss Harmon. She—" He ran to grab the phone as it rang.

"Hello. No, he's not here right now. Who wants him? Oh. Just a minute." He put his hand over the phone and turned to Jenny. "Do you know when Nick's going to be back?"

"Nick's back." He walked through the front door.

"It's for you, and he says he's a prince." Jed's voice was clearly skeptical as he handed the phone to Nick. "I'm going over to Bryan's, okay, Jenny?"

"Be on time for supper," Jenny called after him.

"Murad?" Nick demanded, and Jenny held her breath in anticipation. Was Murad calling to tell them that Witton had been released? *Please let it be true*, she prayed. Adelaide sounded like such a nice person. She didn't deserve all this grief. And neither did Nick, for that matter. His guilt over the situation was eating him alive.

"No, I understand." Nick sounded incredibly tired. His skin was tautly stretched across his high cheekbones, and harsh lines were carved in his lean cheeks.

Jenny swallowed uneasily. Something was wrong. Very wrong.

"I'm supposed to comfort her with that?" Nick bit out. "No. I'll call her. She's my responsibility. You will let me know if . . ." He broke off as if unable to complete the sentence. "Yes. I will. Goodbye." He depressed the plunger on the phone until he received a dial tone and immediately began to punch a series of numbers. Jenny had the depressing feeling he'd forgotten she was even in the room.

"Nick here, Adelaide." His voice deepened. "I just talked to Murad."

He had immediately called Adelaide without even bothering to tell her what was wrong. And something was definitely wrong. Jenny wrapped her arms across her chest. It was all too clear in Nick's rigid stance and his tightly clenched fist, if not in his soothing promises.

Promises he shouldn't be making, Jenny thought uneasily. How could he be guaranteeing Adelaide that she wasn't going to be alone? He couldn't guarantee that the terrorists would free Witton. Unless Nick meant . . . Her skin paled alarmingly. Unless he meant that Adelaide wouldn't be alone because Nick himself would be with her? Jenny swallowed on a rising sense of panic as Nick hung up the phone. He looked so alone. So incredibly vulnerable that she wanted to throw her arms around him and comfort him. But his very aloofness was an impenetrable barrier.

"What happened?" Her question hung in the air between them.

He blinked, looking at her as if surprised to see her.

"Negotiations have broken down."

"But I thought they were eager to trade?" she protested.

"So did we." Nick ran his fingers through his thick hair. "But apparently they had an internal power struggle and the more militant faction gained control. Their latest communication said they want all fifty terrorists released, or they'll kill Don."

"Poor Adelaide," Jenny gasped.

"To put it mildly. She sounded so flat. So dead. And I didn't even tell her how bad the situation really is." Nick clenched his fingers in frustration. "Jenny, she's about had it." His bleak voice tore at her heart.

"There isn't any hope?"

"The only hopeful signs are that they didn't give a deadline for killing Don and that they're still talking to us. Murad feels that that's because the more radical faction doesn't have total control yet and they don't want to risk alienating the moderates in the group."

"That's what's known as cold comfort." Jenny sighed.

"Dead cold." Nick started toward the door.

"Where are you going?" Jenny was unable to stop the query, even though she knew she had no right to question his movements.

"Just out. I need to be alone for a while." Pain lanced through him as he watched Jenny's skin pale at his words. His careless words had hurt her, and he hadn't meant to do that. But then he hadn't meant to hurt Adelaide, either, and look what he'd done to her.

"I'll be back in time for supper." He tried to smile, but his lips felt frozen under the weight of the guilt and disappointment that held him in its grip. Turning away, he hurried down the front stairs. He had no clear-cut destination in mind when he started his car and was vaguely surprised ten minutes later to find himself at the farm.

Belatedly realizing that he was in no fit state to drive, he pulled around the house and parked in front of the barn. Leaning back against the soft leather seat, he closed his eyes and tried to think, but he couldn't banish the images dancing beneath his eyelids. Images of Jenny's white, anxious features as he'd left the apartment. Of Don's laughing face suddenly stilled in death. Of Adelaide's round, homely countenance, blotched and swollen by her grief-stricken crying.

"Oh, God." His voice cracked. "What am I going to do? All my plans . . ." He looked around the neat barnyard in despair. He'd been so sure Murad would gain Don's release. That he'd be free to nudge Jenny's growing attraction for him into love. That he and Jed and Jenny would be a real family. And now . . . He slammed his hand down on the dashboard in frustration.

So what did he do? He forced himself to squarely face the unpalatable question. His options were severely limited. Either he allowed the situation to continue and ran the very real risk of the terrorists suddenly killing Don, or he took steps himself to gain his friend's freedom. And the only way to gain Don's freedom would be to offer himself in exchange. He had no doubt the terrorists would jump at the deal. After all, he'd been the one they'd intended to capture in the first place.

Perhaps he could conceal one of those new electronic tracking devices on himself so that Murad would know where he was being held. Then once Don was safe, Murad could move to rescue him.

Nick sighed bleakly. The chance of his being rescued alive wasn't good, but there was a chance, which was more than Don had at the moment.

Or Jenny. A terrible sense of loneliness chilled him at the thought of her. How could he bear to leave her? He had to, he told himself. For her sake. Before she fell in love with him. He didn't want her to grieve for him if he didn't come back. He wanted to leave her emotionally whole so that she could get on with her life. So that she could find someone else to love. She deserved so much from life. So much that he'd probably never be able to give her. But someone would. He tried to comfort himself with the thought.

A feeling of unnatural calm filled him as he reached his decision. He'd fly to the Middle East, confer with Murad and then exchange himself for Witton. If he came out of it alive, then he'd return and do his damnedest to win Jenny's love. If he didn't, at least he would have left her heart whole to find love elsewhere. But before he left, he intended to make provisions for Jenny and Jed. To make sure that they were well taken care of if the worst happened. Starting the car, he headed back to town. For the first time since Don had been kidnapped, he felt at peace with himself.

"YOU KNOW, JENNY," Nick said, leaning on his rake and giving her a crafty look, "if you were to pave your backyard, you could triple your parking area."

"But if I paved my backyard, there wouldn't be any leaves for you to rake, and then how would you get your exercise?"

"Chasing you around the bedroom?" He looked hopeful.

Jenny knew it wouldn't work. She flipped another rakeful of colorful maple leaves into the huge pile she was making. Because she never ran. All Nick had to do was look at her with that teasing, sensual glint in his eyes, and resistance was the last thing on her mind.

"On the other hand, I probably get more exercise catching you." His eyes twinkled. "Did you know that making love burns three hundred calories?"

"No, I didn't," she said repressively and then, curious, asked, "How on earth do you suppose they measured it?"

"Well…" Nick leaned on his rake and reflectively rubbed his callused palm over his cheek.

Jenny clenched her hand—she could almost feel the prickly sensation of his emerging beard.

"They must have used averages because there's quite a difference."

"Difference?" She dragged her gaze away from the movement of his hand.

"In how one goes about making love," Nick said in seeming seriousness. "Ranging all the way from the 'lie there and think of England syndrome' to you."

"Me?" she parroted, knowing she was going to regret asking.

"Hmm, if three hundred calories are average, then you must burn at least six hundred. You are one hot little—"

"Nick!" Jenny glared at him.

"But, Jenny—" he grinned at her "—it's a compliment."

"Then why am I offended?" she snapped.

"I don't think you are. I think you're simply embarrassed. For such a wild little thing in bed, you're amazingly straitlaced."

"I'd like to straighten your laces!"

"Really? I'm always open to innovative ideas. Especially in bed."

"If you keep up in this vein, what's going to be opened is your head!"

"But, Jenny, if a man can't be frank with his own wife..." His voice trailed away.

What was he thinking? Jenny wondered uneasily. Nothing pleasant from the look on his face. Going off into his own thoughts was totally unlike Nick. He was not an introspective man. At least he hadn't been until that last disastrous phone call from Murad. When he'd come back for supper that night, he'd been different somehow. As if he'd reached a momentous decision. But what decision? she wondered yet again. There was no way to tell because, except for Nick's occasionally seeming abstracted, life had continued much as usual. Maybe she was reading the situation all wrong, she tried to tell herself. Maybe his abstraction was nothing more than worry over Don. Heaven knew there was plenty to worry about.

The banging of the back door broke into her disquieting thoughts, and she glanced up to see Jed walking toward them. A smile lifted her lips at the football he was tossing. She didn't need a calendar. She could tell what season it was by the type of ball Jed carried.

"Hi, Jed." She smiled at him, but to her surprise he simply nodded to her and walked over to Nick.

"Nice afternoon," Jed offered.

"Uh-huh."

"Too nice to rake leaves," Jed continued doggedly.

Jenny continued to rake, puzzled at Jed's actions. Lately his tolerance of Nick seemed to be slipping into honest liking, but this was the first time Jed had actively sought Nick out.

"I could help you rake the leaves later, Nick." Jed tossed his football from one hand to another. "If you wanted to do something else now."

"Such as?"

"I need to work on my pass receiving, and Jenny wobbles when she throws the ball."

"Oh?" Nick turned and looked at her, his eyes lingering on the soft swell of her breasts beneath her rust-colored sweater.

"He means my passes wobble!"

"You can practice your passes on me anytime, Jenny." Nick grinned at her.

"She won't get any better," Jed told him. "But it's not really her fault. It's the way her pectoral muscles are attached to her chest. Because she's a girl, you know."

"I noticed that." Nick nodded.

"I happen to like the way my muscles are attached to my chest!"

"I do, too." Nick's eyes gleamed with devilment. "But the boy does have a point. Distance isn't your forte."

"Then you'll throw me a few passes?" Jed said eagerly.

"Why not?" Jenny muttered. "He tosses his passes around pretty indiscriminately."

"Don't sulk," Nick reproved. "Like Jed said, it's not your fault you're made wrong. You can be the center."

"I don't want to be the center." Jenny started raking again.

"Ah, Jenny, please," Jed urged. "It's more realistic if we have a line."

"Oh, all right." She was unable to resist the pleading in his gray eyes. "I'll be center, but just for a few passes." She walked over to them. "What exactly does the center do?"

"Jenny!" Jed gave her a disgusted look. "Don't you know the position?"

"I know I hold the position of mother, and that entitles me to a little respect."

"Never insult someone who's doing you a favor, Jed." Nick took the football and turned to Jenny. "The center snaps the ball to the quarterback. That's me. Now get down in a three-point stance."

"Three-point stance?" She looked blank.

"Like this." Jed demonstrated, bending so that the knuckles of one hand rested on the ground.

"The things they don't tell you in the baby books." She followed his directions. "Now what?"

"Now we play." Nick leaned over behind her, his hand pressed against her inner thigh.

"Um, Nick," she muttered as his action sent shards of feeling through her.

"The center doesn't talk." His hand rubbed over the crotch of her jeans, and she jerked forward, falling on the football.

"Jenny—" Jed gave her an exasperated look "—that's illegal procedure."

"I'm off my rocker to have ever agreed to this." She turned to Nick. "What are you doing? No, never mind." She immediately thought better of the question. She knew exactly what he was doing. Fortunately, Jed was oblivious to the undercurrents.

"Come on, woman, before we assess a penalty." Nick's fingers bit into her slim waist as he hauled her back into position.

"I'll penalty you," Jenny muttered, steeling herself to the feel of his wandering fingers.

"Give me the ball on the fifth number," Nick said.

Jenny did as instructed, and then the second he'd thrown it to Jed, she turned and tackled Nick around the thighs. Taken by surprise, he tumbled backward into a pile of leaves with Jenny on top of him. She wasn't on top for long. He quickly shifted their position, and she found herself caught between the crackling leaves below and Nick's hard body above.

Tentatively she wiggled, trying to free herself, but his leg anchored her thighs and his hand slipped beneath her sweater to splay over her stomach.

Jenny gasped at the intrusion of his probing fingers. "Nick!" she protested as his hand inched closer to her breasts.

"There's a penalty for roughing the passer, and I'm collecting it." His mouth closed over hers, and his tongue pressed against her lips. The pungent aroma of musty leaves and crushed grass filled her nostrils even as the thrusting heat of his tongue filled her mouth. Sensation piled on sensation as his tongue stroked abrasively over hers, and a low moan bubbled out of her throat.

"What are you two doing?" Jed's resigned tone brought her back to reality with a thud.

Nick raised his head. "I'm getting even for her tackling me."

"She doesn't look like she minds," Jed observed dispassionately. "In fact, I think Jenny likes kissing you."

"Just between us, I think so, too." Nick winked at him.

"Well, you can kiss him later, Jenny. Right now we're playing football."

Jenny got to her feet and dusted the leaves off her clothes, torn between amusement and embarrassment at Jed's observation. He was right, though, she admitted with a total lack of self-deception, she liked kissing Nick Carlton.

And Nick Carlton liked tormenting her, she thought half an hour later. Somehow, in the course of taking the ball, he'd managed to caress her to the point where her fingers were trembling, her stomach was tied in knots and all she wanted to do was grab him and make mad, passionate love to him.

"Excellent, Jed," Nick praised as the boy came running back after yet another catch. "You've got the makings of a first-rate pass receiver, but I think you've done enough for now." He dug into his jeans, pulled out a bill and handed it to Jed. "Buy yourself a sundae over at Sullivan's. You may treat Bryan, too."

"Gee, thanks!" Jed carefully put the bill in his pocket. "Would you put my ball away, Jenny?"

"Sure." She tucked it under an arm and, once Jed had disappeared around the front of the house, turned to Nick.

"Was that offer of a sundae for his benefit?"

"No, for mine. Right now I'd have given him the keys to the Corvette for some privacy. Come on." He grabbed her hand and hustled her toward the house.

Once in the apartment Nick picked her up and sat down on the sofa with her on his lap. He pulled her closer and for a second simply stared into her glowing face, trying to imprint her image in his mind. Slowly, as if savoring the action, he lowered his head and began to brush his lips down across her cheek.

Jenny shivered and pressed closer, wanting a more substantial kiss. She'd already endured enough teasing that afternoon.

Determinedly she unbuttoned his shirt and slipped her hand inside, reveling in the feel of the crisp hair on his chest scraping over her palm. Gently she tugged at the soft cloud.

A small, secretive smile lifted her lips when he gasped as she lightly flicked a flat masculine nipple with her nails. Leaning closer, she touched the tip of her tongue to his chest and was rewarded by his sudden jerk.

"You like that," she said dreamily.

"I like everything you do. But I especially like . . ." He pulled her to him, but before his lips could meet hers, the doorbell rang.

"Ignore it," Nick pleaded. He had so little time left. So little time left to try to cram a lifetime of living into.

Jenny tried to, but it proved impossible. The sound was like a third party in the room, watching their every move.

"I'll have to answer it." She got to her feet and hurried down the stairs. It was a customer who wanted something from the quilt shop, and it was almost twenty minutes later before Jenny was able to reclose the shop and return upstairs to a fuming Nick.

"Sorry," she apologized. "It was Mrs. Prudhomme. She got this idea for a wall hanging during church this morning and couldn't wait to start on it."

"Too bad," Nick bit out. "You're closed on Sunday. Your hours are clearly posted on the door."

Jenny shrugged. "Everyone in town knows I live above the shop, and over the years they've become used to me opening it whenever they need something. She knew I was here. What was I supposed to say, 'I'm sorry, Mrs. Prudhomme, but I'm making love to my husband and I can't come now'? Nick, the woman's seventy if she's a day. Bluntness like that would probably give her a heart attack."

"Or shock her into some consideration. For God's sake, doctors are on call twenty-four hours a day, not shopkeepers."

"I know, I know." She raised a placatory hand. "It's simply habit, but habits are hard to break. Especially other people's."

"The solution is obvious. You'll have to live somewhere else." He pulled her back into his arms.

Somewhere else? She peered up into his annoyed face. Where else? Did he have a particular place in mind, or was he simply making a general observation? She didn't know, and as his lips suddenly met hers, the answer ceased to matter.

12

THE DISTINCTIVE THROB of the Corvette's engine caught Jenny's attention and she glanced through the shop window to see Nick pulling into the parking lot.

She frowned when she saw Jed in the seat beside him. What was he doing home at twelve-thirty on a school day?

She watched as Jed stalked across the parking lot and burst into the shop.

"Are you sick?" Jenny asked.

"Yes, sick to death of her. And I'm not going back, and you can't make me!" His voice rose perilously. "Do you hear, I won't go back."

"Calm down and tell Jenny what happened." Nick's level voice sliced into Jed's anger.

"It's Mrs. Harmon. She said I was a stupid little boy who didn't know my place. But I know enough to know her classroom isn't my place." Jed's voice cracked. "She said I wasn't fit to be around people, and she told me to move my desk to the back of the room away from everyone else."

"What?" Jenny gasped.

"She said I was to sit there and not talk to anyone. But I got up and left," he related with satisfaction.

"And I found him walking along the road," Nick finished the story.

"I won't go back," Jed insisted.

"Are you sure you aren't exaggerating what happened?" Nick asked skeptically. "No one likes to be disciplined, but—"

"That doesn't sound like discipline to me." Jenny put her arms around Jed's thin body and hugged him protectively. "It sounds more like persecution."

"What did you do?" Nick ignored Jenny's outburst.

"I told her that the period of revolution of Venus exceeds its period of rotation by eighteen days, not sixteen like she said." Jed sniffed. "And it does. You can't change physical facts because you're stupid."

"Did you call her stupid?" Nick demanded.

"No, I didn't have to. It was obvious, and I'm not going back!"

"Not right this moment, at any rate," Jenny agreed. "You go upstairs, and as soon as Marge gets back from lunch, I'll go see Mrs. Harmon."

"And do what?" Nick scoffed. "Yell at her? How's that going to help?"

"Do you have any other ideas?" Jenny bit out. "Sweet reason hasn't done any good."

"I'll go see the woman. I'm sure Jed simply misunderstood what she said and overreacted. A little calm discussion and everything will be fine."

"A good dose of arsenic and everything would be better," Jenny muttered.

"I told you, Litton needs a hit man," Jed agreed.

"I'm beginning to think what you both need is a good stiff dose of discipline. But for the time being, you—" he impaled Jed with a glance "—get yourself upstairs, eat and then start studying."

"I can't study. I didn't wait for the homework," Jed said smugly.

"If you have a sense of self-preservation, you'll be studying when I return, young man." Nick's clipped tone apparently convinced Jed he meant business, for the boy turned and tore up the back stairs.

"And you," Nick turned to Jenny.

"I'm too old to be sent to my room."

"But not too old to be taken to your room." His eyes began to gleam. "So see that you behave yourself while I'm gone."

"Behave myself!" Jenny was in no mood for levity. "I'll have you know—"

The chime of the door opening interrupted her, and she swallowed her impetuous words as Nora Fleming eagerly eyed Jenny's flushed face, sensing something being said that would be worth repeating.

"Why, Nick, I haven't seen you since the wedding," Nora gushed. "What brings you away from the farm in the middle of the day?"

Nick turned to Nora, and Jenny hastily intervened before he said something Jenny would be sorry for.

"Are you sure you don't want me to take care of it later, Nick?"

"No, I will. I'll be back shortly."

"Well!" Nora eyed his departing back with annoyance. "He could have at least said goodbye. But I suppose he's in a big hurry?"

"Uh-huh."

"Married life's not all a bed of roses?" Nora probed.

"Rather like life in a small town," Jenny said dryly.

"I suppose." Nora failed to read any personal significance in the remark, and Jenny sighed and prepared to endure Nora until Marge returned and she could escape. Unfortunately, Marge returned at the same time as four carloads of customers, and it was almost two o'clock before Jenny was able to get upstairs to check on Jed. She found him bent over a book.

He glanced up, his gaze going to the doorway behind her.

"Nick hasn't come back yet," she said.

"He's been gone more than an hour." Jed fiddled with his pencil. "Why do you suppose it's taking so long?"

"Maybe he had to wait to see her. She couldn't just leave a class full of students. Or maybe..." She turned to the door as she heard the sound of footsteps on the front steps. Nick appeared a second later, a thunderous expression on his face.

"Did she talk to you?" Jenny asked.

"She didn't talk to me. She talked at me. Everything Jed said was right. She kept prattling on about a teacher always being correct. That's when I went to the principal."

"I tried seeing Mr. Brewster." Jenny grimaced. "He just mumbled about the necessity of children learning to adjust and how he couldn't change students' teachers on a whim."

"I'm not going back," Jed threw in.

"Yes, you are," Nick contradicted him. "However, you aren't going back to that idiot's class. I told Brewster either he transferred Jed, or we were suing the school district for mental cruelty."

"And it worked?" Jenny asked.

"No problem." Nick lied, seeing no reason to tell Jenny exactly how much trouble he'd had talking Brewster out of simply monitoring the situation for the time being. After having had the dubious pleasure of meeting Mrs. Harmon, Nick had wanted to make sure that Jed was safely out of her class before he had to leave for the Middle East because he knew that the woman would never change and Jenny would have a great deal of difficulty convincing Brewster to reassign the boy. Nick certainly had.

"You mean I don't have Mrs. Harmon no more?" Jed demanded.

"Anymore. You've got Mrs. Frank. You'll like her. She was my third-grade teacher."

"Oh, Nick!" Jed flung his arms around him and gave him a hug. "Thank you."

"S'okay." Nick awkwardly hugged him back while Jenny watched them with a feeling of supreme satisfaction.

"I was going to drive up to Geneva this afternoon and see a man about how to prune my fruit trees. There's still time to make it. You want to come, Jed?"

"In the Corvette?" Jed's eyes gleamed.

"With me driving," Nick stated.

"You could let me start it," Jed pleaded.

"I could, but I won't."

"Ah, Nick," Jed wailed as he followed him out. "I gotta learn sometime."

"Not on my Corvette you don't." Nick's words were light in contrast to the heavy sense of loss that filled him at the realization that some other man would be the one to teach Jed to drive when the boy finally turned sixteen.

"Drive carefully," Jenny called after them and then moved to a window to watch as they emerged from the building and crossed the parking lot to climb into the Corvette. Jed was still pleading, if his gestures were anything to go by.

A feeling of deep peace stole through her. At last, the two people she loved best in the world had accepted each other. She froze as the full meaning of her contentment exploded in her mind. She couldn't love Nick. She couldn't. She closed her eyes in dismay. How could she have done anything so stupid as to fall in love with him?

Easily. She sniffed back the self-pitying tears that were threatening to spill over. Nick was an easy man to love. If only he were as easy to understand. She walked over to the couch and sank down on it, her mind a jumble of confused thoughts. Images of Nick's laughing face, his eyes bright with desire, flittered disconnectedly through her mind.

Think, she ordered herself. *Don't react, think.* But what was there to think about? she wondered with grim humor. Her idiocy for ever falling in love with Nick in the first place? There certainly was no future to be considered. She probed the thought like a sore tooth. He'd agreed to their marriage strictly as a favor. Not because he'd been harboring an uncontrollable lust for her for the past twenty-five years.

But he did like her, she argued against the facts. Liked her a lot. He desired her, too. Unfortunately, she'd seen no signs that his liking and passion had deepened into anything else.

If she had, she could have risked confessing her own love. But as it was, she didn't have the right to try to suddenly change the terms of their agreement. That didn't mean she had to admit defeat. Simply because Nick didn't love her now didn't mean he might not come to love her next week or next month. Her spirits rose at the thought. It was possible. She had fallen in love with him with no encouragement on his part. Whereas if she were to actively encourage his liking for her . . .

She frowned at the wall as she considered her problem. How did a woman make a man fall in love with her? By making herself indispensable, she decided. By insinuating herself into his life. By reinforcing the areas where they did mesh. Such as their lovemaking. She could try adopting a more aggressive role. Nervously she tugged at her earlobe. She'd never found it easy to express affection physically, but she could, she encouraged herself. She had to or else run the risk of losing Nick.

But what about Don Witton and Nick's feelings of guilt over Adelaide? she wondered. How did that affect her chances of getting Nick to fall in love with her? Jenny sighed. It was impossible to tell and equally impossible to wait until the mess with the Wittons was resolved. The whole year might pass and Don could still be a captive the way things were shaping up.

"Jenny," Marge called from the bottom of the back stairs, "I need you. A couple vans of senior citizens returning to Elmira from Rochester stopped, and they're buying like crazy."

"Be right there." Jenny gladly shelved her problems and hurried to help.

IT WASN'T until after dinner that she found an opportunity to put her plan into action. Jed was playing in the backyard with Bryan, Nick was sitting in an easy chair reading the paper and Jenny was clearing the table.

She eyed Nick as she finished stacking the plates. His attention was centered on the sports page. *Be aggressive*, she encouraged herself. *You need to begin strengthening the ties between you and Nick, and the sensual one is the strongest.*

Nervously she ran her palms down over her slacks, took a deep breath and went into the living room. Nick didn't seem to notice her. She paused by the coffee table and pretended to rearrange the things on it while watching him out of the corner of her eye. He seemed sublimely unaware of her. She stifled a sigh. Surely she could compete with the sports page.

Gathering her courage, she moved over to him and touched her lips to the hollow behind his ear. The sudden rigidity of his body almost caused her to retreat, but she deliberately concentrated on her love for Nick, letting it overwhelm her natural shyness. Slowly she explored his ear, savoring the polished hardness of the skin. Reaching his earlobe, she lightly bit it, then stroked it with the tip of her tongue. It's salty flavor filled her mouth, and she moved sideways to continue her exploration along the raspy texture of his jawline.

Nick reached out and tumbled her into his lap. Jenny ignored the sound of crunching paper as she wiggled closer to his broad chest. For a second she was content to simply savor the warmth of his body and the feel of his hardening manhood beneath her hips. Then, remembering her purpose, she began to unbutton his shirt.

Nick's lean brown fingers closed over hers.

Jenny forced herself to meet his gaze. There was faint puzzlement in the depths of his eyes. And something else. She took heart from the gleam of sensual excitement she saw.

"What are you doing?" he asked.

"You don't know?"

"I know you're a very reserved person—" he refused to be sidetracked by her attempt at humor "—and you've never made the first move toward me."

She stared at a white button on his shirt as a feeling of acute embarrassment filled her. Why couldn't he simply have responded? Why did he have to analyze everything?

"Why, Jenny?" he asked gently.

"No deep dark reason," she lied. "I simply saw you sitting there and I felt, well, I felt like touching you. You're very touchable, you know."

"Not half as touchable as you are." A feeling of relief washed through him. For a horrible second he'd feared that she was going to say she'd fallen in love with him, and he couldn't bear the thought of hurting her when he had to return to the Middle East. But that he'd shown her the depths of her own passion was good. It meant that she would be more likely to welcome a man into her life after . . . Unable to complete the thought, he got to his feet with Jenny still in his arms. She might belong to someone else in the future, but at the moment she was his wife. It was him she wanted.

Jenny clutched his shoulders to keep her balance. "What are you doing?"

"We're going to explore this sudden urge of yours in more detail."

"Oh?" Excitement coiled through her at the husky note in his voice.

"Yes, oh." He strode toward the bedroom, and Jenny snuggled against his chest, well pleased with her first attempt at aggression.

SHE WAS STILL BATHED in a warm glow of pleasure the following afternoon when Nick stuck his head in the shop door.

"Can Marge handle the shop for about an hour?" he demanded. "Levitson's agreed to come by tomorrow."

"Sure I can." Marge smiled benignly at Nick.

"Thanks, Marge." Jenny tried to sound casual despite her excitement that Nick had come looking for her. She glanced at the clock. "Jed'll be home in twenty minutes. Please tell him there're fresh sugar cookies on the counter for a snack."

"Will do. Enjoy yourself. This gorgeous weather won't hold much longer."

Jenny grabbed her purse from under the counter and hurried toward Nick. It wasn't until they had reached the farm that she remembered the rest of his words.

"Who's Levitson and why's he coming?"

"Levitson's an architect from Elmira who's coming to see where I can put in a garage and what can be done with the house."

Jenny slowly climbed out of the car, trying not to appear too eager. Nick had already repaired the barn and razed the chicken coop as well as a half-dozen assorted outbuildings in various stages of dilapidation. It was a natural progression that he'd turn his attention to the house, although building a garage sounded like more than repairs. It sounded as if he were planning on living here himself. But when and with whom? She remembered his comment about how she shouldn't be living above the shop. Was he planning to move her and Jed out here? Or was he merely getting the house ready for when he'd fulfilled their agreement and moved out of her flat? Was he asking her advice because she was the only woman handy?

Jenny didn't know, and there was no way to find out short of asking. Which she couldn't do. It was one thing to try to subtly convince Nick that their marriage was a great idea and should be continued and quite another to give him the feeling she was trying to trap him into something he wasn't ready for.

Sufficient unto the moment. One of her mother's favorite sayings floated through her mind. Following him into the kitchen, she decided to pretend that this house was being remodeled for her. As if theirs were a normal marriage.

Indulgently Nick watched her peer into the old-fashioned wooden cabinets over the sink. Somehow she seemed to belong here. He could almost see her handing out cookies to Jed. He frowned as his mental image of the boy suddenly included a pair of toddlers with Jenny's bright red hair and his blue eyes. An almost physical pain twisted through him. Jenny's children wouldn't have his eyes. They'd probably have their father's, whoever that might be. Purposefully he forced the haunting images out of his mind. For now he'd have to be content with planning for Jenny's future, and his farm would make a much better home for her than the flat where she was at the beck and call of every inconsiderate customer.

"Tell me what you'd do if money were no object, and I'll work from there," Nick said.

"Well . . ." Jenny glanced around, wondering how blunt to be. The only thing this room had going for it was its size.

"If it helps any, my mother hated this kitchen." Nick correctly read her expression. "Dad was going to remodel it for her, but he died and she moved to Arizona."

"In that case, it's awful. There's no storage, no counter space and very little natural lighting. If it were mine, I'd enlarge those tiny windows, put in new cabinets, a center cooking island and a shower near the back door so when you come in from the fields, you won't track mud through the house."

"Anything else?" Nick scribbled on the notepad he'd pulled out of his pocket.

"I'd rip out the back porch and put in a deck. Oh, and a laundry hookup in the kitchen."

"Hmm." Nick continued to write. "Let's do the rest of the house. It shouldn't take long."

It didn't. By the time Jenny had reorganized the arrangement of downstairs rooms, put in a pitch for opening up the old fireplace in the living room, added a second bath upstairs and told him he should build a cedar closet in the attic, only forty-five minutes had passed.

"How about the front porch?" Nick asked as they were driving away.

"Don't you dare touch that porch. Some of my fondest memories are of sitting with Angie in that old swing your parents had."

"I remember that thing. It used to squeak if you moved sideways."

"You mean every time you tried to kiss that girl you were going with the summer before you enlisted." Jenny laughed. "Angie and I used to hide in the bushes at the end of the porch and peek out every time it squeaked. We got quite an education."

"And now . . . Damn!" He suddenly stopped the car.

"What is it?" She looked up the highway. It was empty.

"There." Nick pointed to the side of the road, undid his seat belt and climbed out, returning a few seconds later with the most unprepossessing specimen of dogdom Jenny had ever seen.

"Here. You hold him." He handed her the animal. "Somebody has undoubtedly abandoned the poor thing."

Jenny accepted the filthy puppy and gingerly set him on her lap.

"Poor little thing." Her heart stirred with pity as she could feel his heart beating like a trip-hammer. Each and every one of his ribs stuck out from beneath his matted brown fur, and there was a festering wound on his left rear leg.

"He's not much to look at," Nick said.

"He's not anything to look at," Jenny amended, not liking the thoughtful expression on Nick's face.

"With a little food—"

"It's going to take more than a few square meals to make this thing into a dog."

"We can't just turn him loose to starve to death."

"Of course not." Jenny glanced down into the animal's liquid brown eyes. "We'll drop him off at the SPCA. It won't take us much out of our way."

"Hmm," Nick muttered noncommittally and said nothing more until they were almost in town.

"You know, Jenny, Jed doesn't have a dog. Every kid should have a dog."

"Hogwash."

"Jed would love him." Nick's eyes lit up at the thought. "And the responsibility would be good for him."

"I suppose," Jenny conceded, still thinking it was a bad idea but unable to resist Nick's very real pleasure at the thought of giving Jed the animal. Nick had come a long way since Jed had been "the kid."

"Then we'll give it to him?"

"You give it to him," she corrected. "I don't want any part of it."

"Thanks, Jenny, you're a good sport." He pulled into the parking lot of the quilt shop.

Good sport? Jenny mulled over his compliment, finding it lacking in almost every respect. She didn't want to be a good sport. She wanted to be gorgeous, sexy, irresistible . . . Ah, well. She sighed. One had to start somewhere.

"Jenny, where've you been?" Jed ran over to the car.

"She was helping me decide how to remodel my farm-house."

"Open the car door, would you, Jed?" Jenny asked.

"Why can't you—" He broke off as he caught sight of the cowering puppy. "What's that?"

"Well you might ask," Jenny said dryly. "Nick claims he's a dog."

"Who's he for?" Jed whispered.

"For you," she replied. "If you want him."

"Me?" His eyes blazed with happiness. "Of course I want him. Thank you."

"Don't thank me. I was all for taking him to the SPCA. Nick's the one who said you'd like him."

"Gosh, thanks, Nick." Jed gave him a look of undisguised love.

"You're welcome, son." Nick said. Then suddenly, as if realizing what he'd inadvertently revealed, his voice became brisk.

"Jenny, let Jed have the dog and I'll run them over to the vet's for a checkup."

"And a bath, I hope." She glanced down at her filthy slacks in disgust.

"We will." Jed hugged the little animal close to his skinny chest. "And, Jenny, if Bryan comes, tell him to wait."

"I will." She stepped back as the car pulled away, her satisfied gaze following it. Things were working out very well between Nick and Jed. Much better than she ever would have expected, given their rocky beginning. Now if it weren't for the niggling feeling of impending disaster lurking in the back of her mind . . . She sighed, hoping she was simply being overimaginative.

13

"I DON'T LIKE the way that animal is sniffing the table leg."
Jenny eyed the little dog worriedly the next morning.

"You don't like the animal period." Nick barely glanced
up from the papers he was reading.

"True, and I'm going to like him even less if he makes another puddle on my carpet." She shot out of her chair and
grabbed him as he inched closer to the table. "Where's Jed?"

"I told him he could go to Bryan's," Nick murmured.
"There's no school today. It's a teachers' planning day, remember?"

"Of course I remember, but then who's going to walk this
thing?" Jenny gingerly held the wiggling animal away from
her.

"I will." Nick got to his feet, but before Jenny could give
him the puppy, the phone rang and he answered it.

"Yes, Bill, just a second." He turned to Jenny. "Would you
mind taking him out? It's for me."

"Of course not." Jenny smiled in relief. For a second there
she'd been afraid that it had been Murad with more bad
news. But she didn't think that someone named Bill,
whoever he was, was a threat to her precarious peace of
mind.

Nick waited until Jenny had left the room before he
turned back to the phone.

"I've been going over the papers you prepared, Bill, and
they're exactly what I wanted. I'll sign them and drop them
off at your office later this morning. You're sure that if

something were to happen to me, there wouldn't be any hitch in Jenny's adopting Jed?"

"None whatsoever. Accidents are considered an act of God."

Accident, hell, Nick thought grimly. *Murder more likely.*

"Nick," Bill said hesitantly. "If traveling in the Middle East is so dangerous right now, why not postpone your trip for a while?"

"Don't worry. I don't expect any trouble," he lied. "I'm simply making sure that my affairs are in order just in case. Thanks for your help. You're an excellent lawyer."

"Anytime. It's a pleasure to work with a client who knows what he wants."

Who knows what he wants. The words echoed in Nick's mind as he hung up. He knew what he wanted, all right. He wanted Jenny. Jenny, Jed and a baby or two. But what he wanted was no longer the question. He couldn't stay in Litton any longer. His affairs were now in order. It was time to redeem his promise to Adelaide and free Don.

Resolutely he dialed long-distance.

"Nick here, Murad. Any news?"

"Yes, all bad." Murad sighed. "The terrorist whose younger brother we were holding was found shot to death this morning."

"Your men?" Nick asked harshly.

"No. Apparently, the group's internal power struggle took a nasty turn."

"What about the negotiations?"

"They broke them off yesterday. They said they're going to try Witton as an enemy to the cause. I'm hoping that it's simply a ploy to put added pressure on us to release all fifty prisoners."

"I doubt it," Nick said wearily. "Murad, I'm coming back."

"No!"

Nick ignored the interruption. "I'll arrange a connecting flight through New York so I can stop and tell Adelaide that Don will be home shortly. Set up a trade of me for Witton with the terrorists. We can go into details when I arrive."

"Listen to me, Nick—"

"No, it's about time I started listening to my conscience. I appreciate what you've already done, Murad, but I caused this mess, and it's up to me to straighten it out."

"You can't, Nick. They'll kill you! They'll—"

Softly Nick hung up on his friend's vehement protests. Everything Murad said was true. But that didn't change anything. He had to go. He had to free them all from the nightmare they were trapped in.

Checking the number of the airline, he dialed it, explained what he wanted and then waited while they checked the schedules.

"I can fly out of Binghamton or Syracuse, whichever will get me there quicker." Jenny heard Nick's words as she carried the puppy back into the apartment.

Fly? A chilling sense of dread poured through her. Fly where?

Nick glanced down at his watch. "Yes. I can make the flight. Thank you." He hung up.

"Are we going somewhere?" She tried to sound casual.

"I am." He started toward the bedroom, stripping off his T-shirt as he went.

Jenny followed him, temporarily sidetracked by the sight of the muscles in his broad back rippling as he crumpled his shirt into a ball and flung it in the general direction of the hamper as they passed the open bathroom door.

She grimaced as the shirt missed. Honestly, maybe she ought to try housebreaking Nick while she was working on the puppy. That is, if Nick was going to be here long enough. Her stomach twisted nervously.

"Where are you going?" she asked, even though in her heart she knew he could only be going to Adelaide. She watched as he grabbed a shirt from the closet and shrugged into it. The sight lit a tiny spark of anger deep in her feelings of dread and confusion. How dare he wear a shirt she'd ironed to go to another woman?

"New York," he confirmed her fears.

"Don hasn't . . . He isn't . . ." she stammered.

"As far as Murad knows, he's still alive. So far," he added ominously. He checked the contents of his wallet, frowned and then asked, "Do you have any cash on you?"

It was the final straw as far as Jenny was concerned. Not only was her husband about to leave her to go to another woman, but he also expected her to finance it. A white-hot burst of anger exploded in her.

"No!" she snapped.

"It's okay. I'll use the banking machine at the airport."

"And whose money will you get?" Jenny demanded bitterly. "Mine?"

"No, mine, dear wife."

"Oh, you do remember I'm your wife," she sniped. "The way you were taking off to see another woman, I thought you'd forgotten."

"No," he said bleakly. "I haven't forgotten. I haven't forgotten anything."

"Maybe you should!" Jenny yelled at him. "Maybe you should remember that I'm your wife instead of wallowing in guilt over a capricious act of fate."

"Adelaide's baby deserves a father," Nick gritted out. "And I'm going to make sure he gets one."

Jenny closed her eyes against the pain that filled her at his words. It had finally happened. Nick was going to offer himself as a sacrifice to Adelaide to replace the husband who was lost to her. And it was all so senseless. Adelaide didn't really want Nick, even though she might accept his offer, feeling that he owed it to her. Especially if Nick had told Adelaide why he'd married Jenny in the first place. Adelaide might feel that, in accepting Nick's offer, she wasn't breaking up a real marriage.

She had to stop Nick from going to New York. She needed time. Time to talk to Adelaide. Time to convince both Adelaide and Nick that there were other ways of handling the problem they faced than by Nick's sacrificing himself. As she watched Nick pick up his flight bag and turn to leave, she panicked.

"Nick, if you go to Adelaide, don't come back here!"

He clenched his fists to keep himself from grabbing her and telling her that he didn't want to leave her. That he loved her. But he couldn't do that. At the moment all that was hurt was Jenny's pride. And it was better if she was furious at him when he left, he told himself. She'd get over him much faster if she believed that he preferred Adelaide to her. Keeping his back to Jenny, Nick picked up the manila envelope containing the papers for the lawyer, opened the door and forced himself to walk down the stairs.

Jenny's breath escaped on a disbelieving hiss as she heard the powerful roar of the Corvette's engine as it pulled away. He'd gone. He'd actually left. The enormity of it hit her with the force of a blow. Her husband had left her to go to another woman. She sank down onto the couch and stared blindly at the wall as tears began to pour unheeded down her ashen cheeks.

How could she have allowed the situation to get so out of hand? She answered her own question—jealousy. She couldn't bear the thought that the man she loved could leave her to go to another woman.

Jenny drew a long, shaky breath and resolutely blinked back her tears. She didn't have the luxury of indulging in a good cry. Jed could return at any time, and the sight of her bawling her head off would upset him. Although probably not as much as finding out that Nick had left without saying goodbye.

But would Nick come back? She remembered both her fears and her ultimatum. Surely he wouldn't take her at her word. He had to come back, she tried to reassure herself. If not because of her and Jed, at least to pick up his clothes.

"Damn!" she swore. She couldn't have handled the whole situation worse if she'd planned it. So now what? She could wait here in the hope that he'd return so that they could calmly discuss Adelaide and what to do about her future. No, she immediately rejected playing a waiting game. She couldn't bear to sit back and do nothing. The love she felt for Nick was too precious to lose by default. It was worth fighting for.

But how? She began to pace across the small living room. How could she fight for his love if he wasn't here? And by the time he returned—if he returned—it might be too late. He might have irrevocably committed himself to Adelaide. He might view Jenny's parting words as evidence that she was releasing him from their agreement. She grimaced as an echo of her shrill tones sounded in her head. Not just releasing him, but thrusting him outside their small family. He could quite easily conclude that Jenny neither needed nor wanted him, whereas Adelaide did.

No, waiting was impossible. She had to go after him. To convince him that their marriage was too precious to throw away. That they could take care of Adelaide and her baby together.

Her shoulders sagged at the enormity of the task before her. She didn't even know Adelaide Witton's address and

New York was a big place. How could she . . . ? She paused as an idea occurred to her.

Nick had been using the bottom drawer of her desk for storing his papers. It was possible Adelaide's address was among them. It was certainly worth a try. She hurried over to her desk.

She pulled the drawer out and emptied it on the floor. A green bankbook slithered out of the pile. Curious, she opened it. There was a single entry of seventy-five thousand dollars made the day after their marriage. She flipped through the rest of the book. It was blank. No more deposits, but more important, no withdrawals.

How had he paid for the Corvette? Or all those repairs he'd been making to the farm? Did he have savings? But if he'd had savings, then why had he married her? There was no way of knowing and she didn't care, anyway. She had to get him back. Then she'd worry about how she'd gotten him originally.

She tossed the bankbook aside and began to rifle through the papers. Halfway through the pile she discovered an empty envelope addressed to Adelaide Witton. Jenny stared at it, hoping the address was current. She looked for the date on the postmark and then looked closer. There wasn't one. The foreign stamp was unblemished. It had never been mailed. Jenny checked the return address. It was simply the name of a company.

Jenny haphazardly began to shove Nick's papers back into the drawer, furiously making plans. First, she'd call the vet to board the puppy, then Sarah to see if Jed could spend the night with Bryan, and last, she'd get a flight to New York. She could plan how to approach Nick and Adelaide on the trip down.

But unfortunately, her mind was still a blank that evening when the cabbie double-parked in front of what Jenny hoped was still Adelaide's apartment building.

Nervously Jenny studied the towering structure. Somewhere in that building was Adelaide and, she hoped, Nick.

"This is the address you gave me, lady." The cabbie broke into her thoughts.

"Sorry." She absently handed him a bill, not even noticing when he didn't offer her any change.

She climbed out onto the littered sidewalk, shivering slightly as the chilly evening air sliced through her thin jacket.

Gathering her courage, she pushed open the glass doors to the lobby. Except for a young couple amicably arguing by the elevator, it was deserted.

Jenny paused in front of the closed elevator doors as she suddenly realized that she needed a key to open them. Frustrated, she stared at the call box to her right, trying to decide what to do. If she called Adelaide to gain admittance, she'd lose the advantage of surprise. But if she didn't call, how could she get upstairs?

The woman, noticing Jenny's hesitation, turned to her and asked, "Something the matter?"

"I just flew in and I wanted to surprise Adelaide Witton, who lives on the eighth floor." Jenny tried to produce a confident smile. "And I can't do that if I have to call her first to gain admittance."

"She a friend of yours?" The young man eyed Jenny, obviously weighing her potential as a burglar.

"Yes." Jenny stretched the truth.

"I guess it wouldn't hurt to let you up." The woman inserted her own key into the elevator and held the doors open.

"Thanks." Jenny gave her a grateful smile and hurried into the elevator before the woman could change her mind. After pressing the button for the eighth floor, she leaned back against the elevator's oak paneling and tried to decide on the best way to approach Adelaide. But by the time Jenny had reached Adelaide's apartment door, she had given up trying for the best approach and was desperately searching for any approach. But her overwhelming fear that Nick was already lost to her made innovative thought impossible.

Raising her hand, Jenny rapped sharply on Adelaide's apartment door and, when no one answered, knocked again. A sense of anticlimax filled her as the door remained discouragingly closed.

She rubbed her aching forehead and tried to think. All her plans had started with her first confronting Adelaide. Now that she wasn't here, Jenny was at a loss.

She glanced at her watch. Eight-fifteen. It was late for dinner by Litton standards but hardly by New York's. Perhaps Nick had taken Adelaide out to eat. Jenny ignored the curl of jealousy the thought engendered.

"You a friend of Addie's?" a thin, wavering voice from behind Jenny inquired.

Jenny turned to see a faded blue eye peeking out from behind an apartment door that had been opened the width of its chain.

"I just flew in tonight and was sure that she'd be home," Jenny said, managing to avoid an outright lie.

"Normally she would be at this time." The blue eye nodded. "But today hasn't been a normal day. My goodness, no. What with that prince fella calling every ten minutes and wanting to speak to that nice Mr. Carlton."

"Mr. Carlton?" Jenny parroted, wondering how Murad had known that Nick was coming to New York. Unless Nick had called him and told him this morning. But if Nick had called him, then why hadn't Murad talked to him then?

"Can you imagine what that prince's phone bill must look like?"

"I doubt he much cares," Jenny said dryly.

"Addie does. She was a nervous wreck. What with all those phone calls and that prince fella telling her that nothing was wrong. But we knew better. Nobody calls halfway across the world every ten minutes just to pass the time of day. Addie kept crying and saying that her husband was dead."

"And was he?" Jenny asked apprehensively.

"Might as well be," the old woman said with ghoulish relish. "I didn't want to leave her alone, so I stayed to keep her company. Then when that nice Mr. Carlton finally did come, he called that prince fella back on the phone in the den. So Addie, she listened on the phone in the living room. Bad business it is."

Jenny swallowed an urge to scream at the way the old woman was dragging out the details and forced a calm response. "Yes?"

"It seems that that prince fella, he found out where them terrorists were holding Addie's husband and he was moving troops into place to try a rescue."

"Oh, my God!"

"And Addie was so upset when she heard that that she went into labor. And her not due till Thanksgiving." The woman heaved a sigh. "She'll probably lose the baby, too."

"Nonsense!" Jenny emphatically repudiated the idea. "It's only a month till her due date, and she'll have excellent medical care."

"That's what that nice Mr. Carlton said. Right after he called an ambulance to take her to the hospital."

"Which hospital?" Jenny hurriedly slipped in.

"City General."

"Thanks." Jenny gave her a harried smile and hurried back downstairs to find a cab. Thirty minutes later she was at the information desk of the hospital. She still wasn't quite sure what she intended to do. All she knew for certain was that she'd feel much better once she could actually see and touch Nick.

"May I help you?" The busy receptionist hung up the phone and turned to Jenny.

"I hope so. Was Adelaide Witton admitted to maternity today?"

"Just a minute." The woman pushed some buttons on the computer in front of her. "Yes, at four-eighteen."

"Has she had the baby yet?"

"There's nothing listed here. Why don't you go up to maternity and talk to them? It's on the fourth floor, left wing."

"Thanks." Jenny gave her a nervous smile and, getting into the elevator, rode it to the fourth floor. She went through a pair of double doors labeled Maternity and down the hall to the nurses' station.

"Excuse me." Jenny addressed an elderly nurse. "Could you tell me if Adelaide Witton has had her baby yet?"

"No." The woman looked up from the chart she was reading. "First babies take quite a while."

"Do you know if the man who came in with her is still here?"

"No, but you could try the waiting room. It's down there." The nurse pointed to the hallway to her left.

"Thank you." Jenny slowly walked toward the sign. She stepped into a small, sterile-looking room, and her heart jumped as she saw Nick. He was sitting on an orange plastic chair, his elbows on his knees and his head bent. Pity twisted through her at the hopelessness etched on his taut face.

"Nick?" she said softly. "Nick, I—"

"Jenny?" He looked up. The sudden blaze of emotion in his eyes at the sight of her propelled her into his arms.

"Oh, God, Jenny, you aren't a mirage, are you?" The longing in his voice brought a lump to her throat.

"I couldn't let you go without telling you that I didn't mean it."

"Didn't mean what?" Nick stared hungrily at her.

"Any of it, but especially the part about you not coming back."

"Where's Jed?" Nick looked beyond her as if expecting to see the boy.

"The Pearsons are looking after him tonight."

"You left Jed to come after me?" he asked incredulously.

"Of course I did." His eyes, particularly when he'd first caught sight of her, gave her the courage to say, "Jed's just my son. You're my husband. Nick, I... You... You can't stay with Adelaide as a substitute for Don. You just can't. I don't care what I agreed to at the beginning of our marriage."

"I wouldn't even try," he said simply.

"You wouldn't?" She blinked, taken aback.

"Nope. If you love someone, there's no such thing as a substitute," he said with utter conviction.

"Then why did you come to New York to see Adelaide?"

"New York wasn't my destination. I simply arranged a connecting flight through JFK so that I could stop and see Adelaide."

"Connecting to where? You only took one small flight bag."

"To the Middle East. To exchange myself for Don Witton. Don't you see, I had to," he insisted at her incredulous expression. "Adelaide couldn't take any more."

"No. No! I won't let you!" Her voice rose hysterically. "I'll stop you. Somehow I'll stop you. I will! I—"

"Jenny!" Nick grabbed her and pulled her into his arms. "Calm down." He rubbed his large hand soothingly across her back.

"Calm down!" she sputtered. "My husband tells me he's about to commit suicide and I'm supposed to be calm!"

"The whole question has become academic." Jenny felt a shudder ripple through his large frame. "Because when I told Murad what I was going to do, he took matters into his own hands."

The phone calls every ten minutes. Jenny remembered what the old woman had said. "What exactly did Murad do?"

"He decided to try to rescue Don. Apparently he's known where they were holding him for days, but he was hoping force wouldn't be necessary."

"Thank God for Murad." Jenny sagged against him. "I know I'm being selfish, but I love you so much. If anything were to happen to you . . ." Her voice was thick with tears.

"Oh, Jenny!" His embrace became a stranglehold, but she barely noticed. "I meant to leave before that happened."

"I'm sorry," she said hopelessly. "I didn't mean to embarrass you."

"You've never embarrassed me. Haunted me, perhaps. Definitely handed me all my fantasies and dreams on a silver platter. I'm head over heels in love with you, woman. I'm surprised you didn't figure it out." He grimaced. "I thought I was being glaringly obvious."

"Not to me." Jenny happily snuggled deeper into his embrace. "Why didn't you tell me?"

"Because I didn't want to hurt you. I knew I was going to have to do something about Don and Adelaide, and I didn't want to leave you with a lot of regrets."

"Yes, Adelaide." Jenny's happiness dimmed considerably. "What are we—"

A harried-looking nurse stuck her head in the door. "Nick Carlton?"

"Yes?" Nick turned and Jenny felt his body tense.

"There's an overseas call for you. You can take it at the nurses' station."

Nick grabbed Jenny's hand and rushed past the nurse.

"And keep it short," the woman called after them. "That phone isn't for public use."

"Carlton here," Nick snapped while Jenny stared at the gray desk top and madly tried to pray. But the only prayer she could think of was "Now I Lay Me down to Sleep," and she didn't like the ending of that one.

She heard the click of the phone being hung up, and gathering her courage, she looked at Nick. The incredulous joy in his face was blinding.

"He's safe?" she whispered, hardly daring to believe it.

"All except for a broken wrist." Nick grinned at her. "When Murad stormed the front of the house, Don's guard went to see what all the commotion was about and Don jumped through the back window and fell a story and a half to the ground. Murad said the bone's being set now and, when the plaster's dry, he'll fly him home on one of their jets. He doesn't want to risk Don standing around a public airport."

"I should think not," Jenny agreed in heartfelt tones. "Let's tell poor Adelaide."

"It'll be nice to be able to give her some good news for a change. Excuse me," Nick addressed the incurious nurse behind the desk. "We'd like to see Adelaide Witton."

"You aren't the baby's father, are you?" She eyed him suspiciously.

"No, but—"

"Have you, at least, had natural childbirth classes?" she demanded.

"No, but I've delivered hundreds of calves."

"Calves!" The woman seemed to swell with outrage. "My dear sir, we deal in babies here. Not animals."

"A mammal's a mammal," Nick snapped back. "Furthermore, birth is a perfectly normal process despite hospitals' attempts to surround it in some kind of weird mystique."

"We are merely safeguarding the mother's health!" The nurse glared at Nick.

"And doing a marvelous job of it, I'm sure." Jenny surreptitiously gave Nick a warning kick in the shins. "Thank you for the use of the phone. If there's any news of Adelaide, we'll be in the waiting room."

She took Nick's arm and all but dragged him back to the waiting room.

"Why didn't—"

"Just a minute." Jenny pulled her wallet out of her purse and checked the contents. "How much money have you got on you?"

"Close to a thousand dollars."

"That should be enough."

"For what? A bribe?"

"No, bail. Honestly, Nick, for a former spy you aren't much on devious methods."

"I told you, I wasn't a spy," he said in exasperation. "I was an intelligence gatherer."

"A rose by any other name." She stuck her head out of the door and peeked down toward the nurses' station. The woman they'd been talking to was bent over her paperwork with her back to them. No other nurse was in sight.

"Jenny, we've got to tell Adelaide."

"And we're going to." She nodded in agreement. "But it could take forever to convince that woman out there to let us in and I don't trust her to deliver a message."

"So what's your plan, Sherlock?" Nick smiled indulgently at her earnest expression.

"We're going to sneak into her labor room."

"And get arrested for trespassing." He suddenly understood her reference to bail.

"Are you with me?" she demanded.

"All the way." His words had the ring of a vow.

"Good." Jenny smiled at him, her love clearly written on her face. "Now all we have to do is figure out which room she's in."

"That's simple. We'll read the names on the charts."

"Charts?"

"Uh-huh." Nick pointed to the small wooden holder beside each of the labor rooms across the hall. "The patients' names are on their medical charts."

"I take it back," she said admiringly. "You make a great spy."

"Come on." With a cautious look toward the nurses' station she crept down the hall. They found Adelaide's chart in the third holder. Taking a deep breath, Jenny pushed open the door and they slipped inside. She blinked in the dim light, glancing around. There were two beds, but only one had an occupant. A thin young woman was lying on her back, and the sound of her muffled sobs tore at Jenny's heart.

"Adelaide?" Jenny hurried toward her.

"Go away, nurse." Adelaide never even looked at her.

"Adelaide, we've got great news." Nick stepped around Jenny. "Don's safe. Murad has him."

"Safe?" Adelaide's tearstained face paled alarmingly.

"Except for a broken wrist." Nick sat on the edge of the bed and took her twitching hands in his. "Murad stormed the terrorists' hideaway, and Don jumped through a window."

"Don always was resourceful." Adelaide's laughter was cut short as she suddenly tensed in pain. "Oh, dear," she whispered, her whole body going rigid. "I'm sorry," she gasped once the contraction had passed.

"Nick?" Adelaide stared into his eyes. "You wouldn't lie to me, would you?"

"No, he wouldn't," Jenny said. "Hi, I'm Jenny."

"It's nice to finally meet you in person," Adelaide said. "As a matter of fact, under the circumstances, it's fantastic to meet you. When will Don be home?"

"Tomorrow. I'll meet his plane and bring him directly to the hospital. So all you have to do is have the baby."

"All!" Adelaide gave Jenny a wry glance. "Isn't that just like a man?"

"Nick has lots of experience." Jenny laughed.

"I tell you, a mammal's a mammal," Nick insisted.

"Let go of her hands!" an outraged voice from the doorway ordered. "You aren't sterile!"

"Thank goodness," Jenny blurted out and then flushed scarlet at Nick's shout of laughter.

"This is no laughing matter!" the nurse sputtered. "The both of you are full of germs."

"Please don't be angry with them," Adelaide pleaded. "They only came to tell me that they've got my husband."

"Well, they should give him back!" the nurse snapped. "A husband should be with his wife at a time like this. And as for you two . . ." She fixed an accusing eye on them.

"We were just leaving." Jenny sidled toward the door.

"Good luck, Adelaide." Nick gave her an encouraging smile. "We'll be in first thing in the morning with Don."

He took Jenny's hand and pulled her past the frowning nurse.

"Whew." Jenny breathed a sigh of relief as they made it to the elevators. "For a second there, I thought we were goners." She pushed the Down button.

"After what we've been through, what's one nurse? I love you, Jenny Carlton. I can hardly believe that I have the right to tell you that."

"Well, you do, and I hope you'll keep telling me that for the rest of our lives." She frowned as she suddenly remembered something. "Nick, there's still one thing I don't understand. When I was looking for Adelaide's address, I found your bankbook with the untouched seventy-five thousand in it. If you didn't need the money, why'd you marry me?"

He shrugged. "There was no one overriding reason for what I did, but rather a lot of little ones," he said slowly. "I liked you as a person; you brought back memories of earlier, happier times; I was used to looking out for you, and since I wasn't having such luck fixing Adelaide's world, I opted to have a go at fixing yours. There was also the fact that I think you're the sexiest woman I've ever met."

"But why didn't you spend any of the money?"

"Yes, well . . ." A dark red tide stained his cheeks. "Remember the business in the Middle East I said was being sold?"

"Yes." She nodded.

"It was my business." He paused. "I cleared about eighteen million on the deal."

"What?" she yelped. "You've got eighteen million dollars! Then why did you take my measly seventy-five thousand?"

Nick shrugged. "Because that way we were equal. You didn't feel you were under an obligation to me for marrying you. But that's enough of the past. It's the future I'm concerned about. Let's go call Sarah Pearson and see if she's

willing to keep Jed for a few days while we have a honey-
moon."

"You're on." She trustingly took his hand and followed
him into the elevator toward a future that beckoned with
shining promise.

Harlequin Temptation

COMING NEXT MONTH

#185 THE LADY IS A CHAMP Frances Davies

Reporter Rainey Archer wasn't dreaming about anything more than her Big Break—the ultimate exclusive. Then Quinn rolled into town, and suddenly she had a new partner, a new roommate, a new best friend . . . and a new fantasy.

#186 THE WISHING POOL Leigh Roberts

Persis Whitley was born to roam, whereas neighboring Missouri farmer Hugo MacAllister didn't even believe in taking holidays. No one was more surprised than Persis when his steadfast love began to temper her wanderlust. . . .

#187 WORTH WAITING FOR JoAnn Ross

In Hawaii, Kara thought she'd finally gotten away from it all—permanently. But then vacationing police captain Adam Lassiter introduced her to another paradise—one he would take with him when he left. . . .

#188 A LITTLE MAGIC Rita Clay Estrada

Marissa hadn't planned on getting pregnant, any more than she'd planned on falling in love with Adam. But she wasn't sure that their marriage was meant to be. Not one to leave things to the fates, Adam set out to convince her. . . .

If *YOU* enjoyed this book, your daughter may enjoy

Keepsake

Romances from

CROSSWINDS

Keepsake is a series of tender, funny, down-to-earth romances for younger teens.

The simple boy-meets-girl romances have lively and believable characters, lots of action and romantic situations with which teens can identify.

Available now wherever books are sold.

Janet Dailey
Americana

A romantic tour of America with
Janet Dailey!

Enjoy two releases each month from this
collection of your favorite previously
published Janet Dailey titles, presented
alphabetically state by state.

Available NOW wherever paperback books
are sold.

Harlequin Intrigue

In October
Watch for the new look of

Harlequin Intrigue

... because romance can be quite an adventure!

Each time, Harlequin Intrigue brings you great stories, mixing a contemporary, sophisticated romance with the surprising twists and turns of a puzzler... romance with "something more."

Plus...
in next month's publications of Harlequin Intrigue we offer you the chance to win one of four mysterious and exciting weekends. Don't miss the opportunity! Read the October Harlequin Intrigues!

**For the millions who can't read
Give the Gift of Literacy**

One out of five adults in North America
cannot read or write well enough
to fill out a job application
or understand the directions on a bottle of medicine.

**You can change all this by joining the fight
against illiteracy.**

For more information write to:
Contact, Box 81826, Lincoln, Neb. 68501
In the United States, call toll free: 1-800-228-8813

**The only degree you need
is a degree of caring**

LIT-A-1R